Further
FENWAY FICTION

Further FENWAY FICTION

More Short Stories from Red Sox Nation

Edited by Adam Emerson Pachter

ROUNDER BOOKS

Published by Rounder Books

an imprint of:
Rounder Records
One Rounder Way
Burlington, MA 01803

This book is a work of fiction. Names, characters, places, and incidents either are products of the authors' imaginations or are used fictitiously. Any resemblance to actual events, places (well, except for Fenway Park) or persons, living or dead, is entirely coincidental. This book is independent of and neither sponsored nor endorsed by Major League Baseball and/or the Boston Red Sox baseball organization.

A portion of all royalties from sales of this book
will be donated to the Red Sox Foundation.

The excerpt from *Tartabull's Throw* by Henry Garfield is reprinted with the kind permission of Atheneum Books for Young Readers, an imprint of Simon & Schuster's Children's Publishing Division. Copyright © 2001 Henry Garfield. *The Tragedie of Theo (Prince of Red Sox Nation)* first appeared in the December 2005 issue of *Boston* magazine. "This Could Be the Year" first appeared on the CD *Red Breath*.

Cover design by Steven Jurgensmeyer
Cover photo illustration by Mary Kocol
Interior design and composition by Jane Tenenbaum

2007929458

ISBN-13: 978-1-57940-143-6
ISBN-10: 1-57940-143-0

9   8   7   6   5   4   3   2   1

This book is dedicated to four now at play in the fields of the Lord:

Ida Pachter, Joyce Miller, Ilse Gjuga, and Constantine Seferlis

and to the keiki now and still to come.

Contents

Further
FENWAY FICTION

Introduction

ADAM EMERSON PACHTER

Shortly after noon on October 27, 2004, I sat in front of a television screen, watching veteran Boston sports reporter Bob Lobel try to remain calm enough to speak. I remembered seeing Bob on TV back in college, and 15 years later, some of his lines ("Why can't we get players like that?") were still the same. But October 27 had brought one thing entirely different: an unprecedented 3–0 lead in the World Series. Even among the superstitious fandom of Red Sox Nation, there was a sense that the curtain was about to fall on the "curse" that had kept this team from true victory for 86 years.

Bob was standing on the field of Busch Stadium, and after he had finished with his report, anchor Liz Walker had one question — in all his years covering the Red Sox, was this the most excited he'd ever been? Bob paused, and I did too, asking myself the same thing. After a moment, he said, "Yes, this is it. This is the top of the hill." That night, under an eclipsed moon, the Red Sox completed their sweep and brought a World Series Championship to Boston for the first time since 1918.

Emotionally I stood next to Bob Lobel on the hill of that bright October afternoon, putting the finishing touches on the manuscript of the first all-fiction anthology devoted to any sports team. That book, *Fenway Fiction,* came out in September of 2005, fortuitously dropped in the midst of a pennant race that culminated with a Sox-Yankees battle for the division title in the final weekend of the season. As it turned out, both teams would be bounced in the first round of the playoffs, and just between you and me and the Green Monster, although I swore at Matt Clement and Tony Graffanino for costing us any shot at another title, my

1

heart wasn't in it. After all, we had our trophy, one that many Sox fans had lived and died having never seen. We had watched millions flood the streets of Beantown, we had felt the weight lift from millions of shoulders. And how could I complain when the White Sox, a team whose losing streak extended all the way back to 1917, took home the 2005 crown? To me, that seemed like poetic justice.

Of course, while the Red Sox 2004 victory did wonders for my psyche, it left me with a bit of a literary problem. As I noted in the introduction to *Fenway Fiction,* all of its stories were composed before the Red Sox won the World Series, and I'm sure that the decades of repeated failure had a lot to do with making the Red Sox such an attractive subject for the writers whose stories I compiled. In fact, while watching the NESN program "What If...," which ran a simulation of what might have happened if Grady had lifted Pedro in the eighth inning of that star-crossed 2003 ALCS game (guess what? the Sox would have won), it occurred to me that on purely selfish grounds at least, it was a darn good thing that the Olde Towne Team hadn't pulled out a victory that night. Without that extra bit of angst, without the fresh dagger that defeat stuck in the Nation's gut, I doubt I would have come up with the idea for the book, nor gotten as many good stories for it.

But now we'd been, in Bob Lobel's words, to the top of the hill, and I wondered what sort of inspiration lay on the other side. Could fiction handle victory as well as defeat?

To my great relief, the answer to that question is yes — a World Series trophy has not robbed Red Sox Nation of everything it wants to say. In fact, victory has taken the sequel in exciting and previously impossible directions, from the new epilogue David Kruh and Steven Bergman are now able to supply for their musical tour through the Curse of the Bambino, to the fresh possibilities Sox fans can now embrace in Tracy Geary's "October 2004." As for my own entry, "Cuttyhunk," it revolves around the fabled World Series Trophy tour, another event that, had it not actually occurred, would probably have been too far-fetched even for fiction. Of course, being Red Sox fans, we still don't like our victories completely uncomplicated, which leads to the peculiar ramifications found in Jennifer Rapaport's "Fallout" and Rachel Solar's "The Bet," both of which might be subtitled, "be careful what you wish for."

And though the 2004 Series might have been expected to put 1986 to bed, I find a few ghosts still wafting through Tim Gager's wicked satire "Fantasy Camp."

Speaking of ghosts, we've got some more in *Further Fenway Fiction*, from the nursing home of Elizabeth Pariseau's "A Little Business, A Little Ballgame," to the Fenway battlements of Steve Almond's "The Tragedie of Theo (Prince of Red Sox Nation)," which provides this installment's slice of Shakespeare (other contributors have mined sources as diverse as Longfellow and Leviticus for their inspiration). And former players like Johnny Damon who are not dead, but merely dead to us, get their due in Mitch Evich's "Johnny Boy." So I guess this sequel proves the truth of Faulkner's adage that the past isn't gone, it's not even past, at least not in the heads of Red Sox Nation.

For those who haven't read the first book, let me repeat my standard disclaimer: all the stories here are fiction, and even where they incorporate real-life Red Sox players (and executives), those people are used fictitiously. This should be particularly obvious in satires such as "Fantasy Camp" and "The Tragedie of Theo," but is true throughout.

As before, my first thanks are to the contributors — all those who helped make the first *Fenway Fiction* such a success, and especially those hardy souls — Jen, Tracy, David and Steven, Beth, Matt, Jon, Cecilia, Mitch, Rachel, and Bill, who anted up again and provided new stories just as good, and in some cases even better, than their first. Additional kudos to Jen, Jon, Sam and Christina, who generously donated their royalties from *Fenway Fiction* to the Red Sox Foundation. Together with my own contribution, we've managed to raise hundreds of dollars for a very worthy cause. Thanks also to Mary Kocol, who has supplied another striking cover photo, and Steve Jurgensmeyer for his expert cover design. To these ranks we have added a talented new squad — Steve, David, Bob, Al, Ron, Lenore, Tim, and Sarah — worthy additions, every one. And I want to single out Henry Garfield, whose trippy *Tartabull's Throw* would have been represented in *Fenway Fiction* if only I'd known about it. I have put an excerpt from Henry's novel in the lead-off spot, and gratefully acknowledge Simon and Schuster's kind permission to reprint it. If you like what you read here, I guarantee you'll enjoy the rest of his book.

More thanks are due to Bill Nowlin and Brad San Martin at Rounder Books for all their help with the first *Fenway Fiction*. As a friend and advocate of the classy Sox great Johnny Pesky, Bill has noted that we perhaps unfairly perpetuate the notion that "Pesky held the ball" in the '46 Series, an assertion that seems unsupported by such evidence as is available (two films of the play and the recollections of both Red Sox and Cardinals players on the scene). While, as I've said, these books are fiction and therefore not bound to the strict rules of historical truth, if you're interested in a full consideration of this issue, see *Mr. Red Sox: The Johnny Pesky Story,* also published by Rounder Books.

I would like to express my immense gratitude to everyone who sponsored or attended a reading of *Fenway Fiction*, especially the traveling cheering squad of my wife Debbie, who smilingly sat through the same schpiel again and again; and daughter Lucy, who lives up to her name. I thank God for them and for the support of my mom Lisa, who barnstormed the book across Western Mass.; sister Gillian, who tried to extend its reach to London; and dad Marc, who alliteratively supplied the sequel's title. I also tip my Sox cap to the valiant BU IP softball team, who know the truth of Cyrano's statement that one does not fight merely to win. And speaking of God, I close with a special shout out to three Yankees fans — Sam, Torry, and Karen — who remind me of Tip O'-Neill's maxim that the Bible calls on us to hate the sin but love the sinner. It's not too late for repentance, guys.

So pull up a chair, Red Sox fans, and enjoy another dose of *Fenway Fiction*. Personally, I'm relieved that victory hasn't stripped the Sox of their significance. How can it, when our once-and-future GM uses a gorilla suit to try and skip town? No, the Red Sox will remain the 2004 World Champions, and they will be fascinating to both writers and fans for generations to come. Maybe they'll win another Series soon, and maybe they won't (although right now the '07 squad is looking pretty good). Maybe the glow from the trophy will eventually fade, and maybe it won't. But the way I see it, we've got at least 83 years left to enjoy the ride.

Adam Emerson Pachter

May 2007, Arlington, Massachusetts

Excerpt from *Tartabull's Throw*

HENRY GARFIELD

AUTHOR'S NOTE: *It is late August, 1967. Despite hitting a home run across the face of the full Moon in his last at-bat, young second baseman Cyrus Nygerski has just been released by the minor-league Beloit Turtles. As a consolation, his manager handed him two tickets to the big club's Sunday doubleheader in Chicago. He has invited Cassandra, a mysterious woman he met in the Beloit bus station that morning, to accompany him.*

Comiskey Park, home of the Chicago White Sox, was already beginning to fill by the time Nygerski and Cassandra arrived, more than an hour before the start of the game. After the tiny stadium in Beloit, Nygerski felt overwhelmed by the spaciousness of the old stone ballpark. Their seats were on the third-base side, a dozen rows behind the visitors' dugout. Players for both teams stretched, played catch in the outfield, swung bats at phantom pitches, and milled about in small groups. Several members of the grounds crew dragged a chain-link blanket around the wide dirt crescent anchored by first and third base, reminding Nygerski of pack horses. People drifted in and began to fill the seats around them.

"Pretty good seats," Nygerski commented. "It's a lot bigger park than Fenway."

"And it's gonna be full of people rooting for the Red Sox to lose," Cassandra told him.

"Not all of us," Nygerski corrected her. "Look."

He nodded, and she looked to her right, toward an old man and woman approaching them from the end of the row of seats. The woman's permed white hair, knee-length blue dress and doughy roundness be-

5

spoke New England winters over a woodstove in the kitchen. The tall, slightly stooped man leading her sported an even more readily identifiable badge of regional affiliation: a Red Sox cap.

"I believe our seats are right next to yours," he said to Cassandra, checking the number on his ticket.

"If so, you're in the right place," Nygerski piped up. "We're Boston fans, too."

"Y'don't say?" The old man's lined face lit up. He turned to his wife. "Hear that, Martha? These folks are rootin' for the Red Sox, too. Looks like we got us a cheering section. Where you folks from?"

"I'm from Boston and she's from Maine," Nygerski said.

The old man's lips drew back from his yellowed teeth in a grin of joy. "Converse McLean, Epsom, New Hampshire," he declared. "This here's my wife Martha. We've been Red Sox fans since the days of Babe Ruth."

"They're going to win," Cassandra said.

"By gawd, I hope you're right, young lady," the old man rejoined, taking the seat next to her. He held out a bony, long-fingered hand; Cassandra grasped it.

"I'm Cassandra Paine," she said. "And this is Cyrus. We don't know each other's last names yet."

The two men reached across Cassandra and shook hands. Martha sat down on her husband's opposite side. "Where in Maine?" she asked Cassandra.

"The boonies. Penobscot Bay area. My little brother listens to all the Red Sox games on the radio. We get the Boston stations over the water."

"I have relatives in Ellsworth," Martha said.

"Really? That's not far from where my folks live." And with that, old home week began. Martha and Cassandra had gotten a good way through their family histories before the old man, bored, turned to Nygerski.

"You hear about Ken Harrelson?" he asked.

Nygerski nodded. He had read about the acquisition of the slugging, outspoken first baseman in the newspaper.

"Has he joined the team yet?" Nygerski asked the old man.

McLean shook his head. "Tomorrow in New York. Which is where we'll be, too."

"Yeah? You're following 'em? Cool."

"Our daughter and her family live in Joliet," Martha McLean explained to them both. "And my husband can't be persuaded to take a trip without it tying in with the Red Sox somehow. So I said we could catch a game here and in New York, and he agreed to the trip. First time we've been anywhere in years."

"First time the Sox have been worth the trouble since '49," the old man said, with a wink at his wife. "You know Larry would've wanted us to be here. And Patrick, too, God rest his soul." He turned to Cassandra and Nygerski. "Larry was my son. Born in 1923, three years after the Red Sox sold Babe Ruth to the Yankees. Boy, not many people remember those days, but let me tell you, before the Black Sox scandal, before everything in baseball started bein' about money, Boston was the class of the American League. Between the turn of the century and the Great War, we won five World Series Championships. The 1918 Series was played in September, a month early, because a lot of the players were going into the service. The Babe was a pitcher then, but he batted fourth in the order. He won three games for us. Next year he played outfield and didn't pitch so much, but he hit 29 home runs. More than anyone had ever hit before. And he didn't even play every day. Oh, you could tell he was going to change the game."

"But they traded him," Nygerski said.

"Sold him!" McLean cried, his indignation surprisingly immediate over a 47-year-old wrong. "Harry Frazee sold him, to pay off a failed theater production. To the Yankees! The Yankees were nothing until they stole Babe Ruth from us. Nothing! And you know what? We ain't won since."

"But what does all this have to do with your son?" Cassandra asked.

A misty look came into the old man's gray-blue eyes beneath the awnings of the years. "My son *and* grandson," he said softly. He looked at his wife, seemingly lost for a moment.

"Tell them, Connie," she urged gently. "They're Boston fans. They'll understand."

The old man licked his lips. "Larry served under Eisenhower in Germany," he said. "It was early 1945; the war was won. The Germans were blowing up bridges as they retreated, and the Americans would have to stop and repair them before marching on to join up with the Russians. Larry was killed helping to rebuild a bridge."

"Oh, gosh, I'm sorry," Cassandra murmured.

"Patrick was a baby. Never saw his dad. And he was too young to remember '46, the year after the war, when the Red Sox finally made it back to the Series."

"Which they lost," Nygerski put in.

"Which they lost," the old man echoed. "Pesky held the ball! Enos Slaughter scored from first on a double, and Pesky held the ball. If he'd made the throw, Slaughter would've been out by a mile. But they lost, and they lost the playoff in '48, and they lost to the Yankees in '49 on the last day of the season, and nothing's gone right since."

Nygerski started to say something, but the old man cut him off. "Patrick," he said, swallowing hard, "was shot down over North Vietnam in March. Two other pilots saw his plane hit the ground and explode."

Wordlessly, Martha McLean reached over and entwined her fingers with her husband's. "So you see?" McLean concluded. "My boy and *his* boy both lived their entire lives without seeing the Red Sox win a pennant. I'm the last one left, and I'm going to be here to bear witness when the Red Sox rise again. I'm going to be here to witness it, for *them*."

Nygerski was too stunned to say anything. Cassandra found words first. "Well, I hope they win it, for your sake alone," she said, patting his upper arm. "And I have a feeling they will."

McLean returned her smile. "The optimism of youth," he said with a sigh. "I hope you're right." They were announcing the starting line-ups, putting the names and numbers up on the scoreboard. The old man took out a game program, opened it up to the scorecard in the center, and began writing in the names of the Boston players.

A roving peanut vendor caught their attention. Cassandra turned to Nygerski. "I'd like some peanuts and cracker jack, but a beer would be nice, too. Get you one?" She stood up.

"Where are you going?" The anxiety she had caused him at Union Station was fresh in his mind. She laughed at his worried look.

"To the concession stand. Do you want a beer?"

"Oh. Sure. Yeah, a beer would be all right. Thanks."

He took note of the heads that turned to follow the short red dress across the row of seats and up the aisle. She moved quickly, gracefully, weaving her way between incoming fans like a Christmas ribbon, until she disappeared from sight underneath the second section of stands.

He didn't see her again until the national anthem had ended and José Tartabull stepped into the batter's box for the Red Sox to begin the game. He had been searching the nearby stands for her in vain; now, at the first pitch, she materialized by his side, with peanuts, two hot dogs and two large beers.

And something else. "Here," she said, when they were seated with their food and drinks. She placed a small square of paper, about the size of a postage stamp, in his hand.

He squinted at it. A white piece of paper with a purple blob on it. "What's this?"

"It's what we talked about earlier," she said, quietly. "It's time you became experienced."

His eyes widened. "Is it...?"

She grinned broadly and nodded. "I may have left my heart in San Francisco, but I brought some of this with me. It's good."

"So...what do I do?"

"Just put it in your mouth and let it dissolve," Cassandra explained. "You can wash it down with the beer, if you want."

"And then what happens?"

"Nothing — for about an hour, hour and a half. Don't worry; you'll know."

Nygerski considered the piece of paper with its purple Rorschach test.

"And you won't be traveling alone," she added, holding up a similar paper square. She winked at him with the eye that twitched, and popped it in her mouth.

Nygerski waited a moment, shrugged, and did the same. It didn't taste like anything. "Aren't I supposed to hear Jimi Hendrix music in my head, or something?"

She laughed. "Anything can happen with acid," she said. "I saw the real Jimi, in June, at Monterey. A bunch of us went down in this old farm truck. We all dropped. It was fantastic."

Nygerski took a swallow of beer and turned his attention to the field, where the Red Sox went out quietly in the top of the first. As Gary Bell took his warmup tosses, Nygerski leaned over toward the old man and peered at his scorecard. "The usual lineup, it looks like," he said.

"Yeah, except they got the old man catching. Elston Howard. Can't get used to him without a Yankees uniform."

"He'll be good for us down the stretch, though," Nygerski said.

"Well, he's been around," Converse McLean grumbled. "I s'pose he's worth having in the clubhouse just because he's got pennant race experience, even though he can't get around on a fastball any more."

"He been playing much?" Nygerski asked.

"Some. We're not strong at catcher. Team's strength is supposed to be up the middle, and look at what we've got. Mike Ryan, Andrews and Smith. Three kids."

"They've done all right so far," Nygerski commented.

"Yeah, but they're young. And young hitters get into slumps. But, by gawd, management seems serious about winning this thing. They brought in Bell, and Howard, and now Harrelson. Be good to have some pop in the lineup behind Yastrzemski. I guess he'll play right field, in place of Tony C."

"No one can replace Tony C.," Nygerski murmured, with a touch of reverence.

"I know, son, I know. But baseball is like life. You've gotta pick up and go on. It'd be more of a tragedy if they gave up, if they didn't replace him, if they played the rest of the season with José Tartabull in right. I like Tartabull, but he don't hit homers and he's got a weak throwing arm. If Tony C. hadn't been hit, he'd be on the bench. Where he belongs."

The home crowd stirred as the White Sox scored a run in the bottom of the first, but Boston came back with two in the third to take the lead. Nygerski kept waiting for the acid to kick in. Periodically he looked over at Cassandra; every half-inning he asked if what was supposed to happen was happening yet. But mostly he watched the ball game, and talked baseball with Converse McLean, and basked in the late August sunshine. Which seemed especially bright today, on the shimmering, emerald outfield. The stadium buzzed noisily, though Nygerski noted that it was only about two-thirds full.

In the fifth inning, Carl Yastrzemski hit a tremendous home run into the right field bleachers to make it 3–1. Nygerski watched the arc of the ball as it soared away from him against an electric blue sky, leaving a vapor trail in his mind. It landed among some empty seats, and a blur of human life scrambled after it.

He turned to Cassandra. He noted the curve of her breasts beneath the scarlet dress, the contours of her legs.... Her lips parted and she smiled that crooked smile at him again.

"They're not hittin'," Converse McLean said, beside him. "Yaz can't do it alone."

In the next two innings, Bell, the Boston pitcher, flirted with disaster constantly. The White Sox managed several hits and walks but did not score. The Red Sox hitters went meekly down, one by one, until Yastrzemski, with two out in the seventh, launched another home run into the right-field stands. This time Nygerski saw the whole flight of the ball like time-lapse photography. He saw the seat in which it would land when it was still in flight, and he saw that a little black kid would win the race for the souvenir. He saw several players emerge from the Boston dugout and clap Yastrzemski on the back as he crossed home plate. It all seemed eerily familiar to him, like he had seen it before. The home run did not surprise him at all. And he knew, somehow he just *knew,* that the Red Sox would score no more runs this day.

"They ain't had a hit since about the third inning, except for those two home runs," Converse McLean said, beside him.

Nygerski turned back to the game with an increasing feeling of dread. And in the bottom of the inning the foreboding in his mind manifested itself, as the Boston defense made an error and the White Sox scored two runs to cut the lead to 4–3. Bell was obviously tiring, but Dick Williams, the Boston manager, made no move to take him out.

The stadium began to swirl around Nygerski, colors blending with noises and smells to assault his senses. The straight lines of iron railings and foul lines oscillated, the planes of grass and outfield walls seemed to breathe, in and out, up and down, like waves beneath a pier. Colors grew brighter. Words in the foam of conversation in the crowd rose up, distinct, and splashed him in the face with new meaning. The percussive sounds of bat against ball and ball against glove backed the symphony all around him.

And the sense of doom was palpable. The brilliant blue of the sky was now dotted with clouds, bright on the upper limbs but dark underneath. The Chicago crowd, silent for most of the game, now buzzed with anticipation. Nygerski knew the LSD was asserting itself in his brain, and he tried to focus on the game despite the sensory overload. Fear prickled the inside of his chest, and he tried to force it down.

The batter hit a high pop fly behind home plate, toward the stands in front of them. Nygerski got a good look at the catcher as he threw off his mask. It wasn't Elston Howard. He knew that Elston Howard was black — the first Negro, in fact, to play for the Yankees, years after Jackie Robinson broke in with the Brooklyn Dodgers. Only the Red Sox had been slower to integrate. But the man who made the catch at the railing was a little too tall and reedy for a catcher, and unquestionably white.

"Wait a minute," Nygerski said to the old man beside him. "Did they change catchers?"

"What're you talking about, boy?" said Converse McLean of Epsom, New Hampshire.

"I thought Howard was catching."

"Who?"

"Elston Howard."

"*Elston Howard*? You mean the old Yankee catcher?"

"Yeah." The stadium bent and curled; now Nygerski felt his mind bending as well. What the hell was going on here? "We talked about him, before the game. Don't you remember?"

"Christ, boy, Elston Howard retired. The Yankees benched him, and he called it quits. Why would that old geezer be playing for us?"

Nygerski pursed his lips. "Let me see your scorecard," he said.

"Be my guest," the old man replied diffidently, and handed it over.

Nygerski scanned the lineups. The White Sox had made several substitutions, which the old man had penciled in. But the Red Sox had made none. And listed in the seventh spot in the batting order was Mike Ryan, catcher.

"I'll be goddamned," Nygerski said weakly. He looked at Cassandra, who smiled at him, her pupils dilated. Her dark hair shimmered against the red dress.

"Enjoying the game?" she asked him.

"Something's wrong," he said.

She smiled enigmatically, her crooked teeth lovely in the sunlight. "I said you'd know, didn't I?"

"This isn't right," he insisted. "Something's changed."

"You better believe it," Cassandra replied.

The White Sox got another hit in the eighth but did not score. Still Williams stuck with Bell. The Red Sox went out in order in the ninth, still leading, 4–3.

Nygerski squirmed in his seat. I'm a ballplayer, he thought. I'm a *good* ballplayer. What am I doing watching this game from the stands? I should be down there. He shook his head to banish the thought. He reminded himself that he had been released from the low minors. What the hell was he thinking?

"Three more outs," McLean said softly, as Bell came out to pitch the ninth.

But the first batter, Ken Berry, brought the crowd to its feet with a double down the left-field line. The noise washed over Nygerski like a wave. "Oh, Christ," McLean muttered, beside him. The next batter was in the batter's box; the noise had not died down. The batter bunted the first pitch toward first base. The Red Sox made the play, but Berry went to third.

He's going to score on a fly ball.

Nygerski looked quickly at Converse McLean and Cassandra, but neither had uttered the words. Yet he had heard them as clearly as if they had been spoken directly into his ear.

He's going to tag up and score, and tie the game.

Nygerski looked around at the people in the nearby seats, wondering where the voice was coming from. But no one had said a word to him.

Cassandra flashed her crooked smile again. "*Now* you're experienced," she said.

The scoreboard announced Duane Josephson as a pinch-hitter for the pitcher. And Dick Williams came out of the Boston dugout, heading for the mound.

"Christ almighty, it's about time," said McLean, joining Nygerski and a few other scattered fans around the stadium in applauding Bell as he left the game. "Pitched a hell of a game, though. The boy put in a day's work."

The reliever was a young Negro named John Wyatt. As he took the first of his warm-up pitches, Cassandra touched Nygerski's arm. "I have to go," she said.

Nygerski actually *felt* his face fall. For a second or two all the muscles, including the ones for speech, simply stopped working. He managed a string of one-word sentences. "What? Now? Where?"

"Home," she said. "It's getting late. I've got to go." She stood up.

Wyatt continued his warm-up. "Cassandra, we've got a game on the line here!"

"I can't stay, Cyrus. I have to go."

She reached into her purse, and pulled out a small, silvery object on a chain. "Here," she said, grabbing his wrist with one hand and placing the object in his hand with the other. "I want you to have this."

"Cassandra, wha —"

But she was already turning to leave. He looked at the gift: a small silver star inside a circle, about the size of a silver dollar. "Cassandra, wait!" he called after her.

Cassandra began pushing her way down the row of seats. Astonished, Nygerski started to follow her. He looked back at McLean and his wife, but their attention was riveted on the field. "Cassandra, wait!" he called after her. The organist played "Charge!" and the crowd roared. The colors of the ballpark swam around him, including a streak of brilliant red making its way down the aisle toward the exit nearest the field.

Duane Josephson stepped to the plate.

"Cassandra!" he called. The red dress and naked legs seemed to dance in front of him as she freed herself from the seats and floated, tantalizingly out of reach, in front of the stands. He looked desperately back at his seat, once, and then at Cassandra, moving away from him. Then he went after her.

He was down behind the dugout, pushing his way through the first row of seats, when Wyatt delivered his pitch. He heard the crack of the bat and saw the spaghetti arc of the ball. The noise of the crowd behind him rose in his ears like wind. The right fielder, José Tartabull, charged toward the ball. Nygerski saw that he would catch it before it fell in front of him, and that Berry, the runner on third, would try to score. Human bodies surged to their feet around him. Nygerski looked wildly around for Cassandra, but he could not see her through the crowd. Someone pushed him forward; he stumbled, and his knee hit the cement hard. Wincing, he struggled to his feet. In front of him, Berry took off for home plate as Tartabull uncorked his throw.

And a ribbon of red, punctuated by long dark hair and fine white legs, moved through the crowd behind home plate, into an opening there that led to darkness underneath the stands. Nygerski's vision filled with her until there was nothing in the stadium but swirling patterns of red, black and white. Ball and runner converged on the plate, on the catcher waiting there at the crux of the impending collision.

The players in the dugout and the people in the stands pressed forward. Berry went into his slide. And Nygerski could see that Tartabull's throw was high, too high. . . . The tall white catcher stretched to get it. He had the ball, but Nygerski saw clearly that his feet were out of position, he didn't have the plate blocked, and the runner would score. . . .

He saw the slide, the catch, the desperate, lunging, sweeping tag, the swirling red dress and long white legs in the dark space behind the plate. The crowd roared as ball, catcher and runner converged in a cloud of dust. He saw the umpire throw his arms out to his sides, and he heard him bellow: "Safe!"

And then all Nygerski could see was Cassandra.

October 2004

TRACY MILLER GEARY

L indy and I managed to get the two last seats at the bar, no small feat considering the game was about to start. I sat down next to a guy with short dark hair who had on a T-shirt that said, "The Curse of the Big Papi." I was wearing a Johnny Damon jersey.

"Another Damon disciple," the dark-haired guy said to his friend, nodding at me. You could tell by his voice that he didn't think I was a real fan of the game, just of Damon.

I shrugged and turned away. It was the third game of the Division Series. The Sox had already beaten the Angels in Games One and Two, and I didn't care what some jerk sitting next to me thought. I just wanted to see the Sox sweep Anaheim.

By the third inning, I learned that the guy sitting next to me was named Johnny, and that the only reason he hated the whole Damon phenomenon was that it made him the butt of jokes with his friends. He looked a little bit like Damon, too, without the stubble and long hair. He looked like Damon might if he ever decided to go the clean cut route.

Once he realized how big a Sox fan I was, he became a lot more friendly. Once I realized how much he looked like Johnny Damon, I became a lot friendlier, too.

Our first date was Game One of the American League Championship Series. We sat at the same bar where we'd met, each wearing our respective Sox T-shirts. A local doughnut shop had been giving out cheap plastic Sox bracelets all summer, and I handed Johnny one I'd picked up for him: Ortiz, #34.

"I've never worn a bracelet before," he said, but he put it on. My left arm was covered with them: Varitek, Schilling, Martinez, Millar, Ortiz, Wakefield, Ramirez, and of course, Damon. I wore them, in that order, for every game. Like any true Red Sox fan, I have a superstitious streak, and it always goes into overdrive in October.

"Did you know this is the forty-sixth time the Red Sox and Yankees have played each other in seventeen months?" Johnny asked.

"That's amazing," I said, though I'd read the same thing in the morning paper.

It was a painful game, with a score of 10–7 Yankees by the third inning. Luckily, the bartender kept the beers coming, so by the time Damon had his fourth strikeout of the game, I hardly flinched.

"You're a real gentleman," I said to Johnny as we watched Damon walk back to the dugout. "You could have given me a hard time about him tonight."

"Hey, we're rooting for the same team, right?" he said.

I leaned my head against his shoulder and he put his arm around me.

"Right," I said.

I watched Game Two with my sister Noreen and her husband Carlos at their apartment in Brighton. Carlos' parents are from Panama, and his whole family worships Yankee relief pitcher Mariano Rivera, who'd shown up in the middle of Game One to take the mound just hours after attending a funeral for two friends in Panama.

"You saw him in last night's game? Rivera?" Carlos said as soon as I hung up my coat.

"He was hard to miss," I said.

"We might not be the best people to watch tonight's game with," Noreen said.

"Don't tell me you want the Yankees to win?" I asked her. I wouldn't have been more shocked if she'd told me that she and Carlos were planning to watch the game in the nude.

"Let's just say I'm tired of rooting for a losing team every year," she said.

I thought about leaving, I really did, but Noreen and Carlos have a 42-inch plasma screen, and my TV at home is a small black and white monstrosity. They work as Special Ed teachers and combined, their salaries are less than half of mine, but they're the ones with the new TV. I settled down onto their couch.

"How was your date last night?" Noreen asked.

"Good," I said, thinking back to the walk Johnny and I had taken from the bar to my apartment after the game, a 10 to 7 fiasco. It had been late and the streets were quiet; it seemed like the whole town was in mourning. As we walked, I kept telling myself, "It's only the first game," and then Johnny stopped in front of the Armani store on Newbury Street and leaned down and kissed me, and I forgot all about the score.

"Good?" Noreen said. "That's all you're saying?" She was anxious for me to meet someone; I could see it all over her face.

"For now, yes," I said. What I didn't tell her: that Johnny had just started his senior year at Boston University, that I'd picked up the tab on our date, and that he was thirteen years younger than me.

Johnny called me at work the next morning. Like most Bostonians, I hadn't gotten much sleep. When I'd finally gotten to bed, after a depressing 3 to 1 loss, all I could hear were Yankee fans taunting Pedro with, "Who's your daddy?" over and over again.

"Wow, you have a secretary?" he said.

"She likes to be called an administrative assistant," I said. I didn't mention that he'd already met Lindy the other night at the bar.

"I don't know about you," he said, "but I'm glad the Sox have today off. If they keep playing this late, I'll never get any work done."

I didn't want to hear what work he was talking about; for all I knew, he had a test later in the day or a paper due. Just thinking about him having schoolwork to do made me feel about a hundred years old. We made plans to watch Game Three together at my place, the following night. But when Friday evening came around, it was pouring in Boston, and the game was cancelled. He showed up anyway, carrying a bouquet of carnations.

"A guy was selling them on the corner of Tremont," he said, handing me the flowers.

"They're great," I said. I waited for him to step inside, but he was busy staring at my entryway. It's a nice space, with an antique table and mirror set I picked up at a flea market over the summer. I'd painted the walls in a black and white checkerboard pattern.

"This place is huge," he said, finally coming all the way inside and pulling off his jacket. "How many roommates do you have?"

"I live alone," I said. "I don't have any roommates."

He gave me a look that was hard to read. I thought he might finally ask me how old I was. It hadn't come up yet, and I look young for my age. But still, he had to realize that I was significantly older than him. I just didn't feel like revealing how *much* older I was. Not yet. And I wasn't sure when I'd tell him I'd gotten divorced just five months ago.

He stepped into the living room. "Cool. A plasma screen," he said, pointing at the 50-inch TV I'd had delivered after work, before I realized the game would be cancelled.

"Make yourself at home," I said. I headed to the kitchen and put the flowers in a crystal vase I keep on display on my windowsill, even though it had been a wedding gift and I know I should give it away.

When I turned around, Johnny was standing right there. I pulled two beers out of the fridge. I handed him one and said, "I thought we could have a few drinks and then head out."

"Or we could have a few drinks and stay in," he said.

The next evening, Lindy showed up at my place right before Arroyo threw his first pitch for Game Three. We ordered Chinese food and drank green apple martinis that she'd made at home and brought over in a plastic pitcher.

"This is the life, don't you think?" she said during the fifth inning. "Martinis, sweet and sour pork, and the Sox are playing the Yankees." The score was Yankees 11, Sox 6. Lindy was originally from Connecticut and I was beginning to think her so-called alliance to the Sox was a ruse to fit in with her co-workers, namely me.

"Life will get a lot better if the Sox actually win this game," I said. I was in a bad mood because Johnny hadn't called all day.

When the Sox were down by eleven runs in the seventh inning, Lindy turned to me and said, "It's more than this game that's got you down, right?"

Lindy is first and foremost my co-worker. I wasn't about to tell her how Johnny had fled my bedroom that morning at the first sign of dawn, or how the only thing he said before leaving was the cliché line, "I'll call you." If he *had* called, his hasty retreat wouldn't have mattered, but he hadn't called all day. I probably wouldn't have minded so much if he hadn't been the first guy I'd slept with since Andrew and I split up, but since he was, I minded a lot.

"It's the game," I said. "That's all." And as the game went on, it was easy enough to blame my mood on what was happening just a mile or so away at Fenway Park. When the game finally ended after midnight, Lindy and I just sat there, staring at the final score on the TV screen. 19-8 Yankees. It was over. As soon as Lindy left, I picked up the carnations Johnny had brought me and threw them in the trash, vase and all.

I spent Sunday at the office, and when I came home I didn't look at my answering machine for a good half hour. The blinking light turned out to be a message from Noreen, who did a terrible job of sounding disappointed by last night's game. She invited me over to watch what she called, "The last game of the Sox season." I deleted her message and didn't call her back.

At game time, I pulled the couch out and made up the sofa bed with my softest sheets. I piled it high with pillows and settled in under my down comforter, bracing myself to see the Sox season end with a whimper. The only thing is, it didn't end. The score was Yankees 4, Sox 3 at the top of the ninth. Rivera was pitching, so I knew Noreen and Carlos had to be in heaven. Then Dave Roberts stole a base, and Bill Mueller got a hit and brought Roberts home. The score was tied, 4 to 4. At 1:22 in the morning, in the twelfth inning, Ortiz sent a ball directly to the Yankees bullpen and the next thing I knew, horns were blasting up and down my street and I was dancing around my apartment, something I couldn't remember ever doing before, and certainly not in the last five months.

I was the only person on time for work the next day. Lindy was a good hour and a half late, but I let it go. I didn't even say anything about the old Red Sox sweatshirt she wore. It had "This is the Year!" written across the chest, but the words were faded, like they'd been washed many times over the years.

At game time, I was back on my sofa bed, surrounded again by every pillow I owned. I barely moved during the entire game, and when it was the top of the eighth inning and the Sox were behind 4–2, I barely breathed. I didn't take a good breath until Ortiz hit a home run and tied the score. In the fourteenth inning, Ortiz got another hit and brought Damon in from second base. The final score: Sox 5, Yankees 4.

Noreen called me two seconds after the game ended. "Did you see that?" she screamed. I wanted to ask her when she'd decided to become a Sox fan again, but instead, I just screamed along with her. Outside, the whole town was awake.

By the time Game Six took place in New York, my superstitions were fully in place. I didn't budge from my sofa bed except to grab a beer or take a bathroom break. It would have been great to talk about Schilling and his bloody sock, or how childish A-Rod looked when he knocked the ball from Arroyo's glove, but the Sox hadn't lost since I started watching the games alone from my living room and I wasn't about to change my routine for anything. When the Sox won 4–2, I knew I'd done the right thing staying home.

The next day I was eating lunch at my desk when Lindy burst into my office.

"Johnny's on the phone," she said. "Do you want to take it?"

I rubbed at my eyes and nodded. I was too tired to feel nervous or angry when I picked up the phone. If I'd expected an apology from him, it was clear he didn't feel bad for leaving my apartment like he had or for waiting several days to call me.

"Can you believe this shit?" he said. "What do you say we meet at the same bar, right after work? This is going to be one great game."

I thought about my living room couch, still pulled out into a bed, all ready for me. I thought about how the Sox hadn't lost since I'd stayed home to watch them. And then I thought about the next day, when win or lose, the series would be over and my couch would still be there.

"Okay," I said. "I'll meet you there."

After Johnny hung up, I called Noreen at work and asked if she and Carlos could meet me for the game.

"You can meet Johnny," I said when she started complaining about how tired she was.

"It's a deal," she said.

Johnny must have shown up at the bar sometime after lunch, judging by the great table he had for us, close to the bank of TVs. He gave me a kiss and pulled my chair close to his. Noreen seemed genuinely happy to meet him, but as soon as he left the table to go to the bathroom, she gave me a sly wink, like I was trying to pull something over on someone.

The whole mood was different this game, and not just in the bar. You could see it on the TV in the faces of the New York fans at Yankee Stadium. The Red Sox had momentum this time around, and even the Yankees knew it. Just after midnight, Sierra hit the ball to Reese, who threw it to Mientkiewicz for the last out. The game was over. The dead silence that had filled the bar during Reese's throw turned into something else, a loud, living thing. Johnny threw his arms around me and I held on tight, screaming along with everyone else in the bar. We ran outside to the street, to the sounds of horns and firecrackers and people shouting. Johnny lifted me high up onto a fire hydrant and held my hips while I tried to balance myself.

I stood high above the crowd and took a good look around. An old man wearing an ancient-looking Sox cap was leaning against a parked car, tears streaming down his face. A young dad held up a little girl no older than three or four years old, her pudgy arms waving in the air. A group of teenagers danced in the light of a street lamp.

"I wouldn't get too used to this," Noreen called up to me.

I didn't know if she was trying to warn me about Johnny, or telling me that this was it, this was as far as the Sox would go. Either way, I didn't care. I just closed my eyes and felt the cool night air, full of possibilities.

Fallout

JENNIFER RAPAPORT

From where I sit, in a little bitty cubicle "outside" the large office with a window, I can hear the masses. They whoop and holler as if no hours have passed, as if they never went home to bed. Some blow whistles and others sound hand-held horns. The ones in their cars honk until either they themselves can no longer stand the sound or they have to make a phone call.

I have to make a phone call. I dial home to Dave, who called in sick. He doesn't answer. I put the phone down and press my fingertips against my eyelids.

My boss, Liz, who is really the department assistant — coffee, smiles, memos for everyone — walks in and I turn to her. She sees I'm upset and rushes to comfort me.

"Oh, no!" she says. "Come into my office."

I do, and when I sit, her plush leather sofa swallows me whole. I glance out the window. Liz sits down next to me, straightens up my shoulders and hands me a tissue. When I tell her that it's Dave again and I don't think I can take it anymore, she exhales through her nose.

"Thank God," she says. "I thought you were taking the other job."

I reassure her and go back out to my desk. I decide that today I like it better where I sit. Through Liz's window, I could see the painted faces, the naked beer bellies, the long-limbed daredevils shimmying up lamp posts. It is not what I want to see. I try Dave again. He answers this time.

"I thought I saw you on a lamp post," I tell him.

He hangs up on me.

We almost lived in the Fenway, too. We would both have been able to walk to our jobs, but it was one of those bed-in-the-wall apartments, and we can only afford to watch the games on TV, anyway. I call Dave again. This time he picks up and doesn't say hello. We sit there breathing at each other until he hangs up on me.

At home in the evening, I tell Dave that I told Liz about us. I don't mention her response, but he lies down on the bed and curls into a ball anyway. He is still in the clothes he slept in the night before. There is no sign of today's paper. And there is no noise in the apartment. No television, no radio, and the windows are shut tight.

"She never liked me," Dave says. He doesn't pick his head up or anything. Sometimes, in profile, he looks like a cleaned-up Johnny Damon to me. He has the same wide jaw, straight nose, long lashes. From the side, you can't see how dark his eyes are, or what's happening to his hairline. "If I'd ingratiated myself to her," he says, "she'd have run the story."

"Untrue," I say.

Last night was the game. *The* game. The game Dave waited for his whole life — longer, he says, than the 86 years his grandfather waited. "I've been waiting longer," he screamed into the phone at the 92-year-old man in the bottom of the eighth. "I've waited my *entire* life."

Last night the television was on, the radio was on, the windows were open, everything. We don't live anywhere near the Fenway, or even in one of those yell-out-the-windows Boston neighborhoods, but we opened them just to listen. We knew the Sox were going to win. Everyone knew. There was no doubt in my mind. By then I had pushed Dave's story far from my mind, and Dave had, too.

The story — Dave's story, the one he wrote about the Curse — had been weighing on us for most of the season. Dave's a writer. It's not his day job, but he's dedicated. For over a year he'd been saying that this was the story that was going to get him published. He was so sure of it that he stopped working on everything else. And it *was* good, too. He gave it to me and I gave it to Liz. She actually put it on the October lineup with a question mark, then bumped it when she realized that October was the month of the Series. (We are not a sports magazine, *per se;*

women's fitness is more like it.) That's what pushed Dave out to the edge. Any earlier in the season and he might have shut down completely. Of course, any earlier in the season the magazine would have bought the story.

"*Totally* untrue," I reiterate. I sit down next to him on the bed. I want to put my arms around him — I really do — but I don't want to give him the wrong idea. We have been through this. "Liz liked it. It was just bad timing."

"Bad timing?" he says. "I gave you that story a year ago. She could have published it earlier if she actually liked it."

I know he doesn't mean this as a stab and that he's just feeling hateful about the rejection, but it makes me feel guilty. And guilt makes me feel bad. Some streak of hot runs up the middle of me.

"Nine months ago you gave it to me," I say. I use my tight-lipped voice. I can't help it. "And you said not to give it to her until you made those changes."

"I made the changes." He's back in a ball now, but his big toes are flexed. They point accusingly at me.

"Not until June. I gave it to her in June."

"May," he says.

"May. Fine. But there's no meeting in May. Not for sports stories."

I hear the phone ringing in the other room, and I know it is his dad; pre-game check-in. The season's over now, of course, but the calls will come for another month, maybe longer this year. It's a ritual that's lasted generations — probably since phones were invented, or since before cars, before families moved away. Not that we've moved away.

Dave was just devastated in June, after the meeting, when he found out the story didn't make it. I told him on a Friday, and he never got out of bed that weekend. We barely spoke to each other in July. I threatened to move out, he threatened to move out. I told him I couldn't take it anymore.

But, then, as the season progressed, so did Dave. He was happy in September — even as far back as August, when nearly everyone pitched in to shred the Blue Jays. I remember, it was Curt Schilling's 16th win, making him second only to Mark Mulder in the American League.

When Ortiz and Ramirez hit back-to-back homers in the third inning, Dave actually got to the phone before his dad called. It was the fastest I'd seen him move in two months. And I thought he was going to herniate something as he screamed the boys home on Cabrera's homer. But when Schilling struck out Gregg Zaun in the seventh, Dave went full bore with the bootie dance. Now, that was unusual. I watched him shake it for two or three minutes — right into the eighth. That was when he must have forgotten about the story, and what a Series win would mean for his "writing career." Instead of being bumped to November, the story would be bumped off the board entirely. But Dave didn't think about it. He didn't even mind going to work in the morning after the win over the Blue Jays, knowing he'd come back to the sound of ball on the television. We watched every game together on the loveseat for the rest of the regular season. Beating the Yankees in the playoffs was like having the perfect wedding. And then the Series was a honeymoon — five days of uninterrupted bliss.

To tell the truth, by Game Three, even *I* had forgotten about Dave's story. And last night — Game Four — we actually decorated the place for ourselves because we knew. We made popcorn and strung it up across the room. We taped our extra jerseys to the wall. We drank beer from plastic cups and listened to "Sweet Caroline" on repeat for over an hour. I even made sugar cookies and frosted them to look like red-and-blue baseballs.

I had just walked back in with the last batch of cookies when Johnny Damon hit a homer on the fourth pitch. Dave shot up from the couch and nearly knocked me over. I planted a kiss on his cheek and closed in to make the most of his gleeful squeeze. Dave leaned into me hard, too, and I really thought that if it hadn't meant taking his eyes off the game, he would have turned to kiss me back. Instead, he put a whole cookie in his mouth and chewed and chewed. Then he wiped his hand clean on my jeans.

We sat tight and close, cautiously optimistic, up until the third, when Trot Nixon hit his two-run double. We were up for a fast high-five, then back down again, and that's when Dave brought up the place in the Fenway again. It was the first place we'd thought about living together — when we had just fallen in love! — so it had a double meaning for us. I nearly choked on the cookie I was eating. I mean, the last two months had been good, but not that good.

"It was half the size of this place," I told him. I didn't know whether to go with the fantasy or be concerned about Dave's mental status. Was he confusing his love of the Sox with his feelings for me?

"But if we were there now, we could roll out of bed tomorrow and be at the Park waiting for the team," he said. He squeezed my hand. I squeezed his back. Deep down, we both knew whose future we were talking about, or at least I did: I could visualize the bus pulling in, Pedro stepping out with that crazy grin on his face.

Dave looked from the screen to me and back again. I glanced at him, too, surprised to see his whole face for a second. Neither of us wanted to miss a single pitch. And then Ortiz doubled and Varitek ripped a grounder to first. Dave looked at me again, and I saw something in his expression that I'd never seen before. It was the same expression my older brother had on his face when he told me his wife was pregnant — a relaxed thankfulness, a giving over to the powers that be.

"I think we should look at it again," Dave said.

I glanced at his profile. Mike Matheny had just tagged Ramirez out at the plate. I waved a hand in front of Dave's face and whistled a little "cuckoo" tune.

"It's long gone, Dave," I said. "That was, like, a year ago."

"Not that one," he said. He pushed my hand away gently. "I mean another one in the Fenway."

"Oh, come on," I said. I elbowed him and took another cookie. "We're happy here."

What I had meant was that we had found a good place, roomy enough, bright, and on the T. I had meant that I had no intention of looking for another place to live. I didn't actually mean that we were *happy,* but hearing myself say it made me wonder: Were we?

What would be the point of living in the Fenway if we never went to the games? I didn't mind taking the T to work, and I wouldn't always be at the same place, anyway. In fact, ever since June, Dave had been after me to get a different job. He even clipped an ad that a local radio station had placed for a broadcast assistant. That was the job I'd mentioned to Liz. I'd never said as much to Dave, but I suspected that the only reason he wanted me to pursue it was so that he'd have a new place to pitch his story. Radio has no lead time.

The phone rang and Dave answered. It was his grandfather.

Things happened to chase thoughts of new jobs and apartments out of my head: Mueller's walk to first, Lowe's unstoppability, Damon's triple, Cabrera's pop-up. I was present for all this, but what brought me back fully was Foulke in the ninth. They brought him in against St. Louis' 3-4-5 hitters; Pujols, Rolen, and Edmonds. We only had three runs, of course, and I was nervous. Foulke hadn't made a save the whole Series. I stood up.

"What are you doing?" Dave said. "Sit down."

"I'm nervous," I said. "I wish they could put Lowe back in." I couldn't sit.

"They can't," Dave said. "He's done his share." He patted my place on the couch, like it was a safe place, a fine place to be.

"I know that," I said. "You think I don't know that?"

Dave pulled me down beside him and held my hand. "Shh," he said. "It's all good."

And then it happened: after Pujols singled, Rolen flied out, Edmonds struck out and Renteria grounded back to the mound. Foulke underhanded it to Mientkiewicz for the third out — and they came together like long-lost friends. So did Dave and I. He picked me up and carried me over to the big window where we waved bandanas at neighbors we'd never laid eyes on before. We cheered out of every window in the apartment, ending up in our bedroom, where we turned on the old black-and-white set we never watch. We finally fell asleep with the windows open and both televisions still on.

I slept through until morning and woke up to the sound of Manny Ramirez. Dave was already up, but still lying in bed. When I pushed close to him, though, he pulled away, as if my body were freezing. His eyes were fixed on the television, as they had been the night before, but his smile was gone. I propped myself up on one elbow to see what Manny was talking about.

"I don't believe in curses," Manny said. "I believe in our own destination."

Dave reached for the remote control and turned off the television. He slammed the remote back down onto his nightstand.

"Hey," I said. "I was watching that."

"It's over," he said.

"What's over?" I didn't know if he meant the broadcast, which clearly *wasn't* over; the Curse, which *was,* but in a happy way; or something else.

"Did you not hear him?" Dave said.

"Jesus, Dave," I said. "Of course, I heard him. The Curse is over. I know. You should be thrilled, not grumpy." I stretched and pulled the covers over me.

"You don't get it," he said.

"Excuse me?" I stuck my head out to look at him. I wasn't ready for meanness after the night we had just had.

"My story," he said. He lay down flat and turned away from me.

"Oh," I said. "That's right." I put a hand on his shoulder, but he shook it away. "But don't worry, Dave. You'll write another one. What else have you been working on?"

"Nothing," he said. I knew he was right.

"I mean, before that."

"Nothing," he said again. "I don't want to talk about it."

"Then what do you want to talk about?" It was as if the Series never happened, as if nothing had happened all summer except me letting him down — except my failure, or his failure. Except all that.

"I don't want to talk about anything." He paused. "I don't want to do anything. I don't want to see anything."

I got out of bed and went to the window. I stuck my head out into the cold and took a hard breath.

"They won, you know," I said. "You know that, don't you? What better thing could have happened?" I couldn't believe this was the fallout.

"You could have taken the other job," he said.

At work two days after the win, as I approach the water cooler, I see the associate beauty editor talking to someone from the art department. They look so much alike that I can't tell who's who. It doesn't matter, anyway; there are no greetings. They smile and look away, as I do. I refill my water bottle and bring it with me to the kitchen.

In the kitchen, I scarf down an enormous cinnamon muffin — the kind no one eats around here except for receptionists and those assistants who lack ambition. My best friend at the magazine is here, too, crying now, instead of me. She's the managing editor's assistant, Amy, and she's been at the magazine two years to my one. Emotionally unstable and ultra-fashionable, she fits in here a lot better than me. I think that she's crying because she's just been lied to or found out.

"It's always one or the other, isn't it?" I say.

She nods and honks her pretty little nose into a tissue, and I decide to stay with her until her problems — work and otherwise — have been resolved.

There is a long pause as we look into our coffee cups.

"Did you ever read Dave's story?" I say. Amy goes to all the issue-planning meetings with her boss. It's probably the best perk of her job.

She slides her PDA out of an invisible skirt pocket and pokes at it with smooth efficiency.

"Yes, I read it," she says. She is suddenly composed, using her no-nonsense meeting voice — the one that originally made me think we'd never be friends. There is no trace of a tear anywhere. "Liz brought it to the October meeting. Too bad Dave didn't send it in sooner. They could have slated it for September."

My spine straightens. I feel physically taller and as if I am tipping slightly forward.

"But we don't run Sports in September," I say. I am sure of this.

"We could," she says. "There's no rule about when Sports goes in. September would have worked."

"It would have?" My heart goes down looking. "She liked it?" I had never really been able to tell if she did or not. All I knew was that she said she wanted to run it, but couldn't. And then the Sox won the Series. Game Over.

"Yes," Amy says. She jots something down with her stylus, then slaps the device shut. "Can we move on?"

"I'll meet you," I say. But when Amy's gone, my throat goes dry and I slide down into a chair at the tiny round kitchen table. I hold small stacks of napkins under my eyes like ice packs. When they soak through, I replace them with new, thicker stacks. I think that without the napkins to absorb the tears, my body would saturate, bloat, and glide down onto the blue-flecked linoleum like the body of a drowned person.

I pull myself together and meet Amy in the stairwell, a place more removed than the kitchen, but also popular with the most obnoxious editors. For this reason we are always careful to leave editorial. We climb either up to merchandising, where the girls are inherently perky, or down to advertising, where they have to be nice. No one is around, so we break open an economy pack of Big Red. As she details her saga, we each chew a piece just until the flavor begins to fade, then pull out the next. When the pack is gone, it is my turn again.

"It's just not working out," I explain, keeping the tears to myself this time.

"Is there nothing I can do?" she says, and I think again of September. I wonder why we never had that conversation before.

I shake my head. "No," I say. It was just bad timing.

She hugs me tight as she can. Somewhere above or below a door swings shut.

"I'll miss you," she says, "when you go."

Cuttyhunk

ADAM EMERSON PACHTER

There was a time, just one, when Annie's father let us raise the spinnaker in the waters south of Robinson's Hole, right when the Cove first bobbed up on the horizon. He hated using it, giving control of the boat over to that one fierce sail you couldn't tack, or jibe, or do much of anything with, really, except be carried along. He hated that huge, billowing sheet that would become such a pain if the wind turned wrong. So he churned out enough excuses that he always had one ready, primed for any occasion. There was never enough time, never enough energy, never enough of a true sou'wester to make it worth our while.

But there's a shift every year in mid-September, a time when you eat dinner with summer and make breakfast in fall. During that brief transition, the haze gets stripped from the cliffs at Gay Head and you can see the colors that August has hidden, shining out there bright and strong. I caught Annie's father watching them from the hill out back of our one real store. And I knew that he'd say yes if I asked him, that this would be that rare occasion when he'd let the spinnaker play its own sweet song.

We pulled it up, Annie and I, grunting with our effort even though it wasn't that hard, nothing seemed hard, not to a teenager. The colors flapped like a moving sunset, and then the wind took the sail and pulled the rest of us with it, gliding like ghosts down the Vineyard Sound, quiet but speedy as we shot along. We were nearly to Nobska before anyone realized that the day was dying, and we still had to turn the boat around. Then the Woods Hole current started playing tricks with us, Annie and I brought the spinnaker down wrong, and by the time we got everything properly arranged, the stars were out and the sea'd turned cold. It was bad enough trying to slip into Gosnold Harbor at noon, rocks all around and the sand bar shifting with each tide. That night we barely made it back to the dock, Annie's father cursing 'til I found the sound that rescued us, WBSM-New Bedford, plucking the Rocket from that Tiger Stadium mound and pulling him across the water until he reached our island home. Clemens was pitching like a god that night, striking men out so fast and furious that he had to be told by the catcher what his right arm had done. Twenty Ks in a single game, a personal best reached twice over the course of ten long years, something no other man had ever accomplished.

That night I also reached a personal milestone — twenty kisses full like spinnakers, bright and colorful as they glided along. We wanted more, reached in for each other. But then there was a sudden splash as we sat there by the harbor, a seagull's caw and the voice of Annie's father. "It's getting late," he said, "and you're off for college in the morning." We were both off, in fact, to different states on different lakes. The wind had shifted, and the moment was gone.

"Nice boat," the man called from the stern of his Alberg 28, spatula-holding hand raised over the grill placed at the edge of his cockpit. I nodded his way, liking the clean lines of his own craft. "Amazing Grace," the stern said. Many days out on the water, it did feel like that.

I didn't let my eyes wander for too long, though. After all, it wasn't the first time I'd gotten that compliment. Everyone loves a Herreshoff, especially the wooden ones. And a 12-footer's just the right size for rigging up quickly and sailing away. The Alberg, well, that would take a while longer to clear her moorings, although on the water she'd likely go twice as fast.

But that wasn't the real reason I kept my glance quick. The real reason was the iPod-wearing 12-year-old at the tiller of my boat, Black Eyed Peas spilling from his ears and disrupting the calm of Quissett

Harbor on a Thursday in June. Don't get me wrong, I liked Fergie and her pals — but if I heard "Let's Get It Started" one more time, I was going to scream.

"Tom," I said. He ignored me.

"Tom!" My student glanced over.

"Enough with the Peas. Keep your eyes on the sail." The wind was behind us, we were almost running wing-and-wing, and I didn't want to get hit by the boom.

Tom looked up and swung the tiller over too fast. I ducked just a step ahead of the jibe.

"Tom," I said, pulling the earphones from his head. "I don't care how your parents drive. You can't handle a boat like a car." He stared blankly at me, so I pushed him over and took the helm.

"Slow corrections, all the time. Like this. Nice and easy, especially with the wind behind you. Do you see how the boom came over quick like that? The mainsail's not going to luff when you're this far off the wind. You've got to look at the jib; it'll cross over first, give you some warning. And remember, you pull the tiller the opposite way you want to go."

Tom was looking at me, but I could tell the song was still playing in his head, blocking out everything I was trying to say. I looked at my watch. Our hour was almost over.

"All right," I said, "take the tiller and head for home. I want your dad to see you steering when we hit the dock. And Tom?" I handed back the iPod.

"Yeah?"

"Nice and easy."

I was lucky; the breeze hadn't picked up yet, and Tom managed a pretty smooth landing. He went in head on, didn't pull off at the last moment, but I'd dropped the mainsail and so we were slow enough that I was able to grab a dock cleat and swing us around. The fenders sighed as we rubbed against them, but Mr. Cavanelli didn't notice the sound. And he was the one signing my checks.

"Looking good, Tom," he said as his son stepped off, leaving me to furl the sail.

"Thanks, Dad." Tom was already back in iPod land.

"Seems like things are going pretty well," Mr. Cavanelli said to me.

"Yes sir; Tom's really improving."

"Well, you do a good job with him." Mr. Cavanelli handed me a twenty. "Thought I'd give you something extra today."

"Thank you, sir; I appreciate it."

"Same time next week?"

"Absolutely. See you then, Tom." The kid was already halfway to his car, but Mr. Cavanelli paused with one more thought.

"So, you gonna see the trophy?"

"Trophy?" I looked up from unclipping the jib. "I thought it already came through Falmouth, back in February." According to the *Enterprise,* they had visited the senior center late one morning, but I was still in class and couldn't get out. There were other stops, up and down the Cape: malls, retirement homes, fire stations. But each time I either heard too late or couldn't make it. I figured I had missed my shot.

"Not here; down on Cuttyhunk."

"They're taking the trophy to Cuttyhunk?"

"Yeah, tomorrow afternoon. Gosnold's the last one. Can you believe it? Already been to every other city and town in Massachusetts, some probably more than once, and it only took them eight months."

Eight months, I thought to myself. Has it really only been eight months?

"You oughta check it out, you know; if the weather's nice."

"Thanks, Mr. Cavanelli. Maybe I will."

Our schools shared a name that showed just how different college would be. Up to then everything had been east for Annie and me: East Coast, AL East — even the storms came from the Nor'east. Now I'd been deposited at Case Western, and Annie was at Northwestern. We had to find our bearings in two very non-Eastern cities. And after a few days I started to think that the whole "try another part of the country for college" idea was seriously overrated, especially since we weren't even at the same one. Both our classes were full of people who couldn't care less about the Rocket and his 20Ks — who saw him as a hated rival, not a pitching god. The only person with whom I could share that incredible memory was Annie, but there's so much going on at the beginning of college — one of us was always out when the other called, grabbing a bite or heading to class. Annie had really gotten into photography the summer before we headed off, and I kept a picture she'd sent me from that final day, a shot of the spinnaker billowing in front of the lighthouse at Tarpaulin Cove. But to my surprise, the picture-taking stayed even as the summer went — Annie started taking classes when she got to school, and most of her darkroom time was at night.

After a month of phone tag, I was getting frustrated. The Sox had finished third, bystanders for the playoffs, so there was no one to root for. But I had it worse — the White Sox were also sitting on the sidelines, but the Indians won their division and nearly 100 games, so I woke up every morning in a city going crazy for another team. Baltimore ended up bouncing them in the ALDS, but it's not like October gave me much to crow about — after all, New York ended up winning it all, and I'll take a bar full of Indians fans over one Yankees cap any day. I didn't have anyone to vent with, so I ended up calling Annie, and after a while she got sick of it.

"Season's over, Ryan," she said one winter night after I was railing about Hentgen taking home the Cy Young. "Time to think about something else."

"But why couldn't they have given it to the Rocket? I mean, his career's almost over, he's won three times with us, he had that incredible game. Why isn't that enough?"

"Ryan, he had a losing record; Hentgen won twice as many games as Clemens did." That was the trouble with dating a woman who knew baseball — she wasn't buying any of my bullshit.

"Still isn't fair," I mumbled.

"Go have a beer," Annie said. "I'm heading to the darkroom."

I hung up the phone and looked at it for a while, trying to picture happy summer Annie. She was right, of course — Clemens didn't deserve to win the Cy Young. But he also didn't deserve to leave Boston like he did — and that was the thing that really hurt, the image of him picking up that bit of dirt from the Fenway mound after his last start in a Red Sox uniform, grabbing one last earthy memento as he was shown the door. I guess I hated the Cy Young going to Toronto because I hated the Rocket going to Toronto just a month later. Who knew that the magic of those 20 strikeouts would only last a few short months?

If I'd kept up like that much longer, I'm sure Annie would have dumped me. But Christmas always cheers my mood, and we had a good mainland time together — the wrapping paper had barely hit the floor from my last present when I was out the door, heading down 195 from my parents' home in Carver to her folks' place in Bristol. I brought her some cranberry cookies and she gave me a kiss right in front of her father. We spent the rest of vacation together, and I barely thought about the Rocket. Besides, the Sox had signed a Cy Young pitcher of their own, Bret Saberhagen, and I couldn't wait to see him in action. By the time spring training started, both Annie and I were feeling good. It was long distance again, though, which meant that most of our communication was again by phone.

In April Annie called me about an hour before the first pitch of Opening Day. "Ryan," she said, "you are not going to believe this."

"What's up?"

"You know that team that plays pretty near my campus, the Chicago Cubs?"

"Sure," I said. I didn't follow the National League much, but everybody knew about the Cubs and how they'd gone without winning for even longer than the Red Sox.

"Well, me and some friends were down at their ball park yesterday, seeing if we could get some bleacher seats for the weekend. And they told us this was the last season for the Cubs."

"The last season? What are they, moving?"

"No, the last season for the name — they're changing it to the Grizzly Bears."

"What?" I clicked off the TV. "The Grizzly Bears?"

"Yeah, apparently they had some contest at the newspaper that owns the team, and people thought Cubs sounded kind of wimpy, so they decided to change it to something fierce, but the football team's already the Bears, so these are going to be the Grizzly Bears."

"My roommate's not going to believe this — he's from Chicago."

"You know, Ryan, if this new name stuff sticks, we better watch out. I mean, who's scared by a team named for red socks? Maybe that's the reason we haven't won in so long."

"I've got to tell my roommate," I said. "Andrew," I called out. "Get your butt in here." As I shouted, my eyes caught the calendar on the wall. "Wait a second. Annie, what day is it?"

"I dunno — first of April?"

"Very funny — I wish I could see your face."

"Ryan," she laughed, "since when has that helped?"

Annie was right; even while telling the craziest joke, she always kept a perfect poker face.

"You win," I said.

"Enjoy the game." She hung up just as Andrew came into the room. "This better be good," he said. "I just topped my high score on Tetris."

"Game's about to start," I said, and then I couldn't stop laughing.

The next time Annie called, it was something more serious, even though she tried to keep the conversation light.

"Hey baby," she said in her best sexy voice, "I've got a surprise for you."

"What's that?"

"You've got to come to Chicago to find out."

"Sure," I said, "one of these days."

"How 'bout this weekend?"

"I can't — the Sox are in town; Sele's pitching Saturday night, and that new shortstop, the one who's taken over from Valentin, is really tearing the cover off the ball."

"Well, I'm sure they play in Chicago too."

"Sure, but not this weekend. Not on this road trip."

There was a bit of silence. "Ryan, I've been to Cleveland twice already this year; you haven't come to Chicago once."

"Well, it's pretty far," I started to say, before realizing that wasn't exactly my best excuse. "Maybe sometime in May."

"School gets out in May."

"Before that then. Look, I'll come see you, Annie. I will. I've gotta go — class is about to start."

I put down the phone before she could say anything more, and felt rotten as I was doing it. The name keeping me from visiting Chicago wasn't Aaron; it was Susan. And she was the one who'd gotten me tickets for Saturday night.

Susan sat two rows in front of me and four seats over. Since I'm a righty, I could follow the arc of my elbow and watch her discretely, all the while still pretending to write. We shared a mandatory science class and a love of baseball, although I didn't know that off the bat. What I knew was that she had model looks and a bright loud laugh that drew attention from across the room. Every time I looked at Susan, Annie seemed so very far away, a summer love too frail to make it through the off-season. Or maybe I was just opening my mind to the fact that there were some awfully attractive women at Case Western.

Whatever the case, I watched her as often as I could, for as long as I could, and wondered how I could arrange to meet outside of class. Then the Blue Jays came to town early in April, and when I saw that the Rocket was gonna pitch, I knew I would be there. His departure had been like a train wreck for the hopes of Red Sox fans, a sudden derailment when we'd been expecting a long smooth ride. Whether you were sitting in the club car or just passing on the highway, when the train jumped those tracks, you had to look.

They called it the "mistake by the Lake," and on a cold Wednesday evening in April, there was nothing to recommend Jacobs Field. Clemens was throwing fire that night, all his passion for winning right there for the world to see. Of course, none of that fire reached the upper decks; I froze my ass off for three innings before deciding to get out of the wind and try to find something closer to the field. Luckily, the city hadn't awakened from its winter slumber yet, and there were plenty of seats along the third base line. I got to mine just in time to see a pretty ballgirl make a great cross-the-body snag of a foul ball before it could conk a freckled six-year-old on the head. As she handed the kid the ball that had almost brained him, I caught a nice long look. It was Susan.

The next day I decided I would go up after class and tell her what I saw, but when I closed my notebook, I was astonished to find Susan already standing next to me.

"So you're an Indians fan?" she said.

"W-why do you say that?"

"Only the diehards at the Jake last night. Bit too early for the rest of town."

"Actually, I went to see Clemens pitch."

"You're from Toronto?" Her look said the only thing stranger than an early-season Indians fan was someone rooting for the Blue Jays.

"No, I'm from Massachusetts."

"Ah, jilted lover." She gave that great laugh. "No wonder you were out there in the cold. Hoping you could catch his eye?"

I laughed, enjoying the banter. "Surprised I caught yours, actually, what with your saving six-year olds from line drives and all."

"Oh that," she smiled. "That was just reflex. Crack of the bat, I'm all action. Rest of the time, I just scan the crowd."

I blushed a little. "Well, I'm glad I got your attention."

"Most of the poachers do," she said. Now I was red in earnest. "Why don't you come back again sometime, my treat. I can get you seats just a couple rows back. And afterwards, maybe I could arrange a little tour. Did you know there's a couch in the clubhouse where only pitchers can sit?"

"Really," I said. "I'd like to see that."

"Well, now's your chance. The Red Sox are coming to town this weekend; I'll leave you tickets for Saturday night."

I tried not to think about Annie as I approached the park. She had called again, ostensibly to make light of our last conversation. It was no big deal, she said; there would be other chances, I wouldn't want to miss the Sox in their first swing through Cleveland, and so forth. The questions seemed innocent at first, but then she got to the clincher, and I made the mistake of answering before I realized what my answer would reveal.

"So, do you have decent seats?"

"Oh, they're great. I'm along the third-base line, just a couple rows off the field."

"Nice," Annie said. "How'd you score those?"

I paused a little too long. "I, uh, have a friend who works at the park. Did you know there's a couch in the locker room that only pitchers can use?"

Annie ignored the bait. "So, is it someone from the sailing club?"

"Uh, no, just a friend from my astronomy class."

"What's her name?"

I swore inside. "What makes you think it's a girl?"

Annie snorted. "Because you're trying so hard not to mention her name."

"Look, Annie, it's not a big deal — it's just someone I met in class who offered to get me tickets. It's not a date," I declared, wondering how convincing that sounded. "She's going to be on the field working."

"So what is she — a member of the grounds crew?"

"No, she's a ballgirl."

This time the silence was way too long. "Must have a nice uniform then," Annie muttered. "Short skirts and all."

"I hadn't noticed." Another lie. "Come on, Annie, I'm just going to see the Sox play."

"Who're you going with?"

"What?"

"You said she got you tickets, and she'll be working during the game. So, who're you going with?"

She had me. "Um, I was just going to go alone."

"So it is a date," Annie said, and then she hung up the phone.

Once I got Annie out of my head, it was a great game, and I could see why everyone was raving about this Nomar kid. From my seat, I could see right across to the shortstop, and Garciaparra put on a great show that night, knocking the first pitch he saw into the bleachers and then ranging impossibly far into the hole to grab a hard grounder. The way he was running flat out, I thought Nomar would bowl Susan over, but he snared it just in time, then turned and leaped as he threw, nabbing the runner by half a step. Even some of the Indians fans cheered that one.

Of course, most of the time my eyes were fixed on Susan, and while she may not have shown Nomar's range, she was still nimble enough to draw my attention. With every move, even just a few steps after a foul dribbler, her skirt would swish and give me a higher glimpse of her toned legs. To be honest, after a while it didn't matter who was on the field, or at least the part between the lines. My eyes stayed riveted on Susan, and when she looked up from time to time and flashed a short sweet smile, I felt the kind of butterflies that I thought lived only on Cuttyhunk. After a few innings of that, I didn't care who won — I just wanted the game to be over.

Of course, Susan couldn't just hop in the stands as soon as the players left the field. She went with them, doing whatever chores were needed once the game was done. I sat in my seat and watched people move slowly out of the park. Fans always move more slowly when the home team's won; I guess people are reluctant to leave the victory behind. And despite Nomar's personal heroics, the Indians had won. So I waited for what seemed like an hour, scrunching down in my seat so the ushers wouldn't evict me. Just when I thought she might have forgotten, Susan returned to the field, and she picked up right where Annie had left off.

"So, you here by yourself?"

"Yeah — not too many Sox fans at school," I said.

"Maybe a few Indians, though." She smiled at my embarrassment. "No, I'm glad you came alone. That's nice."

I smiled, not sure what came next.

"Well, what are you waiting for?"

"You mean, I can just step down on the field?" I'd never done that before.

"C'mon, Ryan, it's not made of gold. All the players have gone home now, and there's just a reporter filing copy in the press box. They'll rake this stuff over good tomorrow — no one will even see your prints."

I swung my legs over the padding at the field's edge and stepped down. Susan took my hand and led me towards the dugout. The dirt felt softer than I expected, nothing like a Little League diamond. I walked by the third base bag and noticed the scuff marks from players running by, little cleat marks visible against the white. Gingerly I kicked up a little chalk, then looked around to see if anyone else had noticed.

"You're such a virgin," Susan laughed. "Don't worry, they'll put down more of that stuff too. Now follow me; let's go find that couch."

If the field had seemed hallowed to my novice feet, the dugout certainly wasn't. The area underneath the player's bench was covered with spat-out flecks of chewing tobacco, mashed-up plastic cups, and empty wrappers. It didn't smell that good, either. But Susan pulled me on, through a tunnel with worse odors and into a cramped room with a row of green lockers and a heap of dirty towels. Over in a corner I saw a couch that would have fit in a frat room, stains competing with tears to see who could do more damage to the fabric. The remaining color on the couch was a faded orange, made darker by the thousands of feet that had put their cleats up there.

But Susan didn't mind. She sat right down and winked. "Have a seat, Ryan."

"I thought only pitchers could sit there," I said.

"Well, then I guess you'd better show me some high heat."

I may have been a dugout virgin, but I'm no fool. I sat down right after she said that, and then I kissed Susan just as hard as I could.

It was great — everything was great and the kind of blurry that comes from having some truly naughty fun. We both had our shirts off, but I wasn't prepared to get fully naked on that nasty couch, so after we finished making out, Susan took me in her car back to campus, and she didn't even wait for an invitation when we reached my dorm.

"Where's your roommate?"

"I'm sure he's over at his girlfriend's."

"Let's go, then. Time to finish what we started."

She took my hand and I couldn't stop staring at her, beauty shining through the blurriness, so I didn't really register anything else until we opened the door of my dorm room and I saw a woman crying there. It was Annie. My roommate had let her in. She didn't wait for anyone to let her out.

The wind came up overnight, and when I got down to the Quissett Harbor on the morning the Sox trophy was scheduled to make its way to Cuttyhunk, the waves were already slapping against the side of my boat. Well, not my boat; technically it belonged to the Yacht Club, but one of the perks of teaching sailing was that they let me take the Herreshoff out for free. And my schedule was clear that day, so I didn't think they'd mind me running down the islands, just so long as I had her back by 5 o'clock. I knew the sea well enough, even though I hadn't been to Cuttyhunk since the night Roger Clemens tied his own strikeout record, the night Annie and I kissed and got ready for college. The summer of '96 I was also teaching sailing, sleeping on a cot in the basement of the island's only pizza joint. Annie's folks actually owned a place — and a sailboat that was even more impressive. That was how we met, in fact; I admired her dad's boat, we started talking, and pretty soon he had signed her up for a few lessons.

"I want Annie to learn sailing, but I can't teach her that."

"Why not? You're a good sailor."

"I'm her dad. She won't learn from me. You teach her."

I agreed because I liked her dad and hoped to get a ride on his boat, but once I saw Annie walking down the dock, all tan and trim in a blue tankini, I got a whole different motivation on my mind. "First lesson's on me," I said, "and I'll teach her for as long as you like." That was during the All-Star Break, three days with few distractions. By the time the Sox started up the second half, Annie and I were inseparable, and she'd sneak down to my basement to listen to the evening games. We kissed a little, but Gosnold's only a blip of a town, and someone always knows where you are, even in a basement. So we kept things easy, just in case her dad ever showed up. I loved it there, holding Annie while the light flickered from the basement's one lamp and the game ebbed in and out — depending on the wind, and the island's generator, and whether someone was trying to dry their hair that night. I could have come back to Cuttyhunk again and again, as long as it was Annie's place, the spot where she and I would sail and smile together.

But after the break-up, I stayed away, looked for work on the Cape instead. As it turned out, the first place that offered me a job was the Quissett Yacht Club, and I'd been there every summer since. Sometimes in the afternoon, I would sail out into the Bay, tacking back and forth in the wind shadow of the Weepeckets. I knew Cuttyhunk was down there at the end of the chain of Elizabeth Islands, but I couldn't see it, not from where I sailed, and even though I hadn't been able to rid my mind of Annie, out of sight seemed to be the proper distance.

Over time, I found that I was keeping baseball out of sight as well; from time to time I'd switch on the TV and start to watch a game, but the cameras would eventually pan the dugout and I'd start thinking about that couch and the look on Annie's face, and then I'd turn it off. In 1999 and 2003 I caught the playoffs — I mean, I couldn't avoid that — but both times Clemens stuck the knife into us, sitting there all cocky in his pinstripes. Didn't matter that he got shelled at Fenway in '99 and knocked out of the pivotal Game Seven four years later — his team had won, and his team wasn't the Sox.

I'd hear that clip of his over and over in my mind, that stupid sound bite where he said he had to go to New York to win a trophy, and it hurt because it was a gratuitous slap, sure, but also because the truth hurts, especially when it comes from someone you loved. For me, Clemens and Annie and Cuttyhunk were like those three linked rings that magicians use. They're separate circles, isolated bits of metal, but then the magician knocks them against each other and — boom — they're all joined at the center, at the strongest spot. Now you can't imagine them apart any more than you could have imagined them together, and when the magician finally does pull them back, there's nothing but air in the space that used to hold your heart.

The two best things about Herreshoff 12s are that they look good and are tough to sink. The good looks got me plenty of compliments in the harbor, but once I entered the white-capped waters of Buzzards Bay, the seaworthiness became more important. It was one of those days where the Cape and Islands were much cooler than the mainland, with our steady southwest wind blowing off all the haze on the other side of the Bourne Bridge. Of course, that same wind made for rough seas, and as soon as I took my first tack outside the harbor, a wave crest slapped against the hull and covered me with spray. It looked like I would have to fight the wind all the way to Cuttyhunk, but I didn't really mind. Salt water's better than coffee for a morning jolt, and this time I had the boat to myself, with no iPod-wielding teenagers to distract me. The boat started tilting a little in the wind, but I kept myself planted, balanced on the side opposite the sail and looking for any gusts that might push me too far over.

My sailing students always gave me strange looks when I told them to watch for wind, and I guess you grow up thinking of a breeze as something to be felt. But on the water, any gust will ripple the top of the water it passes, so you have plenty of time to brace yourself for a strong blow. Not that I had much to worry about; the Herreshoffs were wide and sturdy, with heavy keels almost impossible to dislodge. I'd probably have my mast ripped off before the boat flipped over, and the seas weren't nearly strong enough for that. So I mostly just sat back, took in the view, and took on the spray. Buzzards Bay was pretty quiet on a Friday morning; none of the weekend sailors had gotten off work yet, so I had the views almost entirely to myself. New Bedford's factories poked into the horizon, but I liked the closer sights — the shallow dunes of the Weepeckets, home to a solo picnicker and hundreds of hungry seagulls; an abandoned bunker carved into a hill on Naushon; the rush of oncoming current as I passed the entrance to Robinson's Hole. I took it all in and thought about the irony that I was sailing to my rendezvous with the World Series trophy, since I'd also been sailing the day of my favorite baseball memory.

I guess it was inevitable that the '04 season would suck me back in. I tried to stay away, told myself that Grady-Bleeping-Little was the last straw. But the clubhouse seemed so loose and confident under new manager Terry Francona, and come August they went on a winning streak like you wouldn't believe. With Kevin Millar cracking jokes and Big Papi crushing homers, the Red Sox roared into September, and I stopped fighting my urge to change channels or switch off the radio. They wouldn't catch the Yankees — not in the regular season at least — but they kept my interest, and so when school started up again, I no longer snapped when my English students gabbed about the game instead of focusing on their assignments. I watched the celebration after they clinched the Wild Card, clicking a beer bottle against the TV screen even though all they'd won was a chance to compete in the post-season — nothing assured, nothing guaranteed. When they actually beat the Yankees in the ALCS rematch, I called my folks just to confirm they'd seen what I'd seen — it was all so exciting and unreal, like if you didn't check it with someone else, then maybe it never happened.

But the World Series was real enough, and by this point I watched every pitch. Seeing them celebrate on the field at Busch Stadium, seeing them pass that champagne-soaked trophy around, I felt the smiles creep back into my relationship with the Sox. I drove up to Boston for the championship parade, cheering with the massive crowd on the Common as Manny rode by in a Duck Boat waving a sign that read "Jeter's playing golf — this is better." It sure was.

I didn't see the trophy on that day, but when Larry Lucchino pledged that he would take it to any town in Massachusetts that made a request, I figured it would only be a matter of time before I got my personal meet-and-greet. But they don't let junior English teachers at Falmouth High skip class for events like that, and every time the trophy approached, something got in the way. It toured Bourne's town hall while I coached volleyball, stopped in at a Chatham senior center while I monitored detention, and slipped into Falmouth during Introduction to Shakespeare. After a while, chasing that trophy started to feel like chasing the World Series title, so I gave up and focused on my work. But then school got out, I returned to my summer job, and Mr. Cavanelli gave me the inside scoop on the trophy tour's last stop. Now Gosnold was bobbing up and down on the horizon, maybe a half-hour's more sailing against the wind. I was about to make my return to Cuttyhunk.

There are certain sounds you expect when you're sailing: the flap of the jib, the slap of water against the hull, the seagulls as they caw. But a helicopter isn't one of them, and that's why I was baffled when I first heard the thump-thump-thump coming over the stern. I glanced around, but there weren't any other boats, and it was right over me before I thought to look up. I'd never seen a helicopter land on Cuttyhunk before, but if they can set down on the top of a New York skyscraper, then I guess the flat lawn of Gosnold's only B&B isn't so hard to figure out. The helicopter touched down just as I tacked into the harbor, dodging the same sandbar that had vexed sailors for a hundred years, and wending my way through the mooring of the island's real residents. Summer folk might use them, but the moorings were never theirs. No, that took living here year-round. And it looked as if virtually all those residents were lined up neatly on the hill, waiting for Larry Lucchino to emerge from the helicopter with the trophy in his hand.

I tied up my boat at the far end of the dock and walked up the hill just as Lucchino was coming down, holding a shiny piece of metal that shone like a lighthouse. The only other time I'd seen all of Cuttyhunk's people together was at the last of the summer's weekly movie nights-and they always picked "Jaws" for that, just to poke fun at the Vineyard. I recognized most of the older faces and few of the younger ones — even on an island, it didn't take long for a new generation to be born. Lucchino placed the trophy on a glorified card table set up just a stone's throw from the door to the basement where I used to sleep. By unspoken agreement, both the very young and the very old got their chance to touch it first, while the rest of us waited. There were a few other Sox employees standing around — I'd read that the trophy had its own security guard, but he must have felt the threat on Cuttyhunk was pretty minimal, because he held back and let the residents smile, and touch, and laugh, and share stories as they took their turn examining a piece of hardware that hadn't visited the state since 1918.

"Did you know our year-round population's 86?" I heard one fellow say, a salt-stained Sox cap pulled down close across his forehead.

"That's our lucky number too," Lucchino laughed, then stepped back to let the next person in line have their private moment.

It might have been an hour before I got to the front of the line, and that was the first time I had a really good look at the trophy — before I'd been focused on the faces of the people around it. There was old Sam Garfield, lobsterman and harbor master, rubbing its side like he wondered what was underneath; behind him Pam Jane, the teacher with the two first names, huffed like she was about to give a pop quiz. I knew them, but I'd been away for long enough that they didn't remember me, and I didn't press the issue, settling for little nods instead of handshakes. To tell the truth, I felt like I'd pulled up on an unfamiliar beach, not sure whether it was public, and I could settle in — or private, and someone was going to come and kick me off.

But then I got up to the trophy, and all the other thoughts washed out of my head. There was more gold than I expected — on TV it looked mostly silver, but up close what really drew you in was the gold trim on the base and the ring of gold-topped pennants, one for every team. A couple of them were bent, casualties of Johnny Damon passing the trophy to some disciples in the St. Louis crowd on the night they won it all. But even that seemed right; our path to the Series had been full of struggle, and a picture-perfect trophy wouldn't have reflected all the years it took to get here. Looking at the trophy, I thought to myself, You see, Rocket, you didn't have to go to New York to get one. You could have stayed here.

And no matter what he said, I knew that the 26th Yankees trophy couldn't be as special as our first — well, at least our first since my grandfather was born. You should have stayed, Roger, I thought — you should have made a deal and put that Fenway dirt back down. Then you could have been here with us now.

"Would you like your picture taken with the trophy, sir?" I shook off the daydream, turned around, and saw a woman wearing a Red Sox jacket, face behind an enormous camera.

"Sure — thanks." I didn't know whether to touch the trophy or not, so I stood there awkwardly, hands at my sides, until she finished the shot.

"Nice day for a spinnaker ride, don't you think?"

I blinked as the woman pulled the camera from her face. It was Annie.

How could I have missed her? Even with the trophy and all this crowd, how could I not have noticed? Annie looked the same, beautiful and smiling, happy like the spinnaker ride almost eight years ago, not like the last time I'd seen her. As we talked it seemed as if time had skipped right over that bit of pain — she was the same, and I was the same, as we'd been so long ago. The tears, the untidy departure, were gone like a gust of wind, and now the water between us was calm again. She asked about my teaching ("it'd be great without all the students"), and then I asked about the Red Sox.

"So you're the team's official photographer," I said.

Annie grinned. She'd just finished taking a group picture of the trophy with every man, woman, and child spending June on Cuttyhunk, plus a couple dozen more that looked to be over for the day.

"Yep, that's me."

"You must spend a lot of time at Fenway."

"Yeah, I'm pretty well-connected. Even got my own office there." She smiled mischievously. "I could give you a tour sometime when the team isn't around. I hear there's a couch in the locker room that only pitchers can use."

I winced at the sudden memory, but she touched my arm as if to say she meant no harm. "Don't worry, Ryan; it's all water under the bridge now. We were kids then, and besides, compared to some of my other boyfriends, you still look pretty good."

"Thanks," I said, trying to think of something other than that smelly couch in old Jacobs Field and Susan taking off her clothes beside it. "S-still can't picture you working for the Sox, though."

Annie nodded. "Well, it wasn't just the Sox; I mean, the photography came first. I ended up switching my major and all — I just loved shooting pictures. After graduation, I spent the summer in Boston, working at Uno's and taking classes over at NESOP. One day I saw this ad on the school bulletin board: 'Photographer Wanted,' and giving the address as 4 Yawkey Way. Went up there with my portfolio, and they hired me on the spot. I shoot all the player photos for the Jumbotron and the official Sox program, plus a little freelance on the side for baseball card companies. A lot of my time is spent working with Wally, though; I mean, he's probably my main client."

"Wally..."

"The Green Monster. Yeah, that's right. His schedule's booked tighter than most of the players — at least they sometimes get an off-day. It seems like Wally's on the charity circuit 24-7: visiting hospitals, senior centers, schools — you name it, Wally's been there. And I'm right there with him, taking photographs. We spend much more time together, people are going to say that we're lovers."

"But he's not here today..."

"Twisted his ankle leading a cheer. Good thing, too — this way he won't see us. For a monster, Wally's pretty jealous."

I looked at her, then laughed. Same old Annie, always saying ridiculous things with a poker face. It was nice.

I wanted to ask her more questions, hear about the trophy tour, learn where she lived, but we were interrupted by a tired man in a Sox uniform who'd been standing nearby. "All right folks," he said. "Everybody had their chance to touch it? Everybody got their picture snapped? Good." I looked at him, wondering how many times he'd given that little speech. I'd read that the trophy had traveled more than 30,000 miles so far, and the man looked like he'd been there for all of it. He picked up the trophy and headed down towards the pier.

"Well," Annie said, "I guess it's time to go. Trophy's got one more stop to make today, and I've got to pick Jason up by 6 o'clock."

"Jason," I repeated, my face falling. So she was married. Things weren't the same, no matter how much I'd foolishly hoped they might be. But why no wedding ring? They say guys don't check, but I did. Her hands were clean. Maybe it was only a boyfriend — still pretty serious, if she was going to pick him up.

"Yeah," Annie said. "The day care charges 20 bucks for every 10 minutes you're late. What a rip-off, huh?"

"Jason," I echoed dumbly. "Your son."

"Yeah, he'll be four in September. Already loves the Sox, if you can believe it. Well, maybe not so hard to believe. I work there, after all."

"But you're..." My throat hurt.

"No," Annie said with a shrug that made me realize how often she'd been asked that question, "we never got married. Chris and I met senior year and kept dating through the summer after college. One night we had too many drinks and not enough protection. Thing is, when I found out I was pregnant, I was kind of glad — I always hoped I'd be a mom someday, and that day just came a little sooner than expected. But Chris didn't want me to keep the baby, and I did. End of discussion. I haven't seen him since... but Jason, he's a great kid. I bet you'd like him. I take him to games wearing his signed Big Papi T-shirt, and everyone at Fenway gets such a kick out of that."

"Annie," a man called from the chopper. "We've got to go."

"I thought the trophy was going back by boat."

"It is; I'm not. They're stopping at some senior center in Fall River, but I've got to get to day care and..."

"Sure."

"I don't have any paper on me," Annie added. "Just a few extra rolls of film. But you can call me at the ballpark. Just dial the main line and they'll put you through." She touched my arm again and started to walk away.

"I think you and Jason would really hit it off," Annie said. "I tell him about Roger Clemens all the time, and that night he got those 20 strikeouts."

"Sure," I said, throat still raw. I tried to picture her child, the little version of Annie whose life I'd never known, never even anticipated. But all that kept coming to mind was Tom Cavanelli and his stupid iPod, oblivious to everything I was trying to say.

I walked down to the dock, hearing the jingle of the jib as it twisted in the breeze. I tried not to think about whether I would call Annie. The helicopter took off from the lawn in back of the B&B, rising towards the Vineyard before banking hard and moving in the direction of New Bedford. The day-trippers and Red Sox personnel climbed on board the ferry, and it began to steam away. All the Cuttyhunk kids stood in a line on the dock, ready to jump in the water as soon as the ferry turned out of sight. I watched them for a moment, then stepped on board my boat and felt it roll gently beneath me. The wind had shifted, and the moment was gone.

Epilogue to
The Curse Is Reversed

A MUSICAL

with
Book and Lyrics by David Kruh
Music and Lyrics by Steven Bergman

AUTHOR'S NOTE BY DAVID KRUH: *The first book of Fenway Fiction contained an excerpt from a musical I had written with composer Steven Bergman about the so-called Curse on the Boston Red Sox since 1920, when Harry Frazee sold Babe Ruth to the New York Yankees. Between late 1997, when we began writing the piece, and April of 2001, when The Curse of the Bambino premiered at Boston's Lyric Stage, we would occasionally have to face the prospect that the Red Sox might break the Curse and actually win it all. That wouldn't be good for two guys writing a musical about decades of hardball frustration.*

Now some years our fears ran higher than others, of course. Like in 1999 when Pedro came in to pitch six innings of relief in Cleveland and Troy O'Leary did his impression of Roy Hobbs from The Natural and Boston went on to the ALCS where, in Game Three against the Yankees, they shellacked their former ace, Roger Clemens 13–1. Other years, like 2000 when the Sox didn't even make the playoffs, were easier on our nerves. But whether the Sox went out with a bang or a whimper, Steve and I held true to a little ritual. As the last out dropped safely into an opponent's glove or the opposing team's winning run crossed the plate, I would pick up the phone, call Steve, and say "Well, we still have a musical."

Funny thing, as opening night for the musical approached, and we found

55

*ourselves inundated with interest from the media, one of the most-asked
questions from the newspaper, radio, and television reporters was, "What
will you do if the Red Sox win it all?" Now the director of our show, Spiro
Veloudos, (a man filled with such passion for the Red Sox that the night in
1986 that Bill Buckner let that ground ball go between his legs Spiro
punched a hole in the wall of a local hotel) liked to reply, "Well, if they do
win, it will be because of this play!"*

*My reply was more practical, based as it was on those yearly phone
calls: "I guess I'll have to write a new ending."*

*But in the spring of 2001, with the possibility of a Red Sox champi-
onship months in the future (and long after the run at the Lyric would be
over) I wasn't giving that a lot of thought. I was having too much fun
watching my very first script being performed at an Equity theater. Even
more of a thrill was when the musical's run at the Lyric was extended two
weeks and ended up becoming the biggest hit in that theater's history.
Though Steve and I would turn our attention to other projects, we continued
to hold a fond place in our hearts for our most successful work to date. We
watched when it was later performed by a regional theater, whose director
and cast gave new perspectives to our characters, and were thrilled when
sales of the original cast CD performed well.*

*Meanwhile our annual phone calls continued. It came, sometimes, at
the end of dramatic seasons — like 2003, when Grady Little kept that same
Pedro too late into the seventh game of the ALCS against the Yankees, and
several innings later Aaron Boone did his own Hobbs-ian impression, send-
ing Red Sox fans' hopes sailing away into the cold Bronx night. More often
than not, though, the call was made in September, since the Sox didn't even
make the playoffs for three years in a row.*

*As I watched the bottom of the ninth inning of the fourth game of the
2004 World Series unfold, I knew the clock was ticking on The Curse of the
Bambino Musical, and I was going to have to follow through on that new
ending. Now, Steve and I hold no illusions about the production appeal of
our story of the Red Sox' frustrations now that a brand new World Series
banner sails over Fenway Park. But we agreed that the right thing to do
was to update the musical's original ending, in which our proto-typical Red
Sox fan watches the sixth game of the 1986 World Series while he cradles*

his infant daughter, whom he had taken from her crib with the Red Sox up by two runs so that she "can tell your children you saw the Red Sox finally win it all." Then he watches, in horror as two hits, a wild pitch, and a badly-played ground ball later, hopes are dashed for another year.

Now, it appeared, that this WAS the year. I remember writing the words in my head as I watched the Cardinals go down one out, then two. As Edgar Renteria, the Cardinals' last hope, stepped up to the plate, I knew exactly how the new ending would go, and I resolved to write it the very next day. But what I could not bring myself to do was pick up the phone and call Steve. This would not be an easy tradition to dispose of. But like a good creative partner, Steve stepped in where I could not go. Seconds after Keith Foulke cradled Edgar Renteria's soft grounder and tossed it to Doug Mientkiewicz, it was my phone that rang.

"Well, I guess you'll have to write that new ending."

"It's already done, Steve," I replied.

And here it is, our gift to all the Red Sox fans who dreamed of that moment. Enjoy.

EPILOGUE

(The lights rise, and we are where we began, in the Father's house with the blue glow of the television illuminating the set. The Rooters, in their raccoon coats, stand upstage holding pennants that say 2004. The father, also wearing his raccoon coat, sits on the couch holding a telephone. He has aged appropriately)

ANNOUNCER

Welcome back to our broadcast of the 2004 World Series. It is 10:35, Central Daylight Time on October 27th, 2004, and you're looking at a live picture of the moon in total eclipse over Busch Stadium here in St. Louis, Missouri, a sight astronomers tell us has never happened during a World Series game. But then, this postseason has been filled with the improbable — no, with the impossible coming true. It's the bottom of the ninth inning, with the Red Sox leading the Cardinals three to nothing. There's two outs, and the Cards have a man on first.

FATHER

You still there? How are you holding up? Me too. I just can't bring myself to get too excited, yet. Remember we were one strike away in 1986 — twice — and still couldn't do it.

ANNOUNCER

Incredible to think that just for the Red Sox to get to the World Series they had to come back from a three games to none deficit against their rivals, the Yankees, an improbable comeback that began by beating Mariano Rivera, arguably one of the great relievers of his time. In Boston they are already etching the names of Kevin Millar and Dave Roberts in granite. Millar for his walk and Roberts for his steal in Game Four of that series . . .

FATHER

You know, it seems like only yesterday I was holding you in my arms right here in this living room, telling you how you were going to see the Red Sox win their first World Series. That was 18 years ago. Yes, I know I've told you the story before. Indulge the man who's paying that college tuition of yours?

ANNOUNCER

After a disastrous outing against the Yankees Curt Schilling — their ace — had to have his ankle surgically stitched into place so he could pitch again. Which he did twice, winning once against the hated Yankees and then against these Cardinals.

FATHER

Someday you'll get married and have your own family and you'll do for your kids what my dad did for me, and Gramps did for him — you'll teach them this game. You'll tell them the stories. The heartbreaking defeats. And maybe now the occasional victory.

ANNOUNCER

Here comes Foulke's pitch . . .

FATHER

Hold it . . .

ANNOUNCER

It's a soft grounder up the middle . . . Foulke one-hands it . . . tosses it to Mientkiewicz . . . and there it is! After 86 years the Red Sox are the World Champions of baseball.

(The Rooters hug each other for joy. Tears begin to well up in the father's eyes)

FATHER

(After a brief pause) Yea, I'm still here. (Wipes tears from his eyes) I am. Well, I guess because I'm thinking about my dad. All those opening days and he never got to see this, you know? (Another pause) That's a nice thought. Maybe he can. (Watches the TV) Look at them. I wonder if they realize what they've done. How they've changed everything. For us. For Buckner and Aparicio and Pesky and Galehouse. (A pause) Yes, even for Grady. (Pause) Because none of that matters now. We can say "World Series Champion Boston Red Sox."

(The father realizes that the Rooters are standing behind him)

FATHER

Honey? Can I call you back? No, everything is fine. Everything is wonderful. There's just something I have to do. Love you, too. Congratulations to you, too, sweetheart.

(The father hangs up the phone, and crosses to the Rooters, with whom he shakes hands and exchanges hugs. Then they all stop to listen to the TV)

ANNOUNCER

In just a few minutes we're going to take you into the Red Sox locker room where the Commissioner will hand the World Series trophy to the Boston Red Sox. We'll take a time out while I let those incredible words sink in.

SONG — So Many Years Ago (Reprise)

FATHER & ROOTERS

FOR MANY YEARS WE LIVED AS THOUGH THERE WAS A
  CURSE
WE ALL ASSUMED THEY'D FIND A WAY TO LOSE

IT WAS BAD LUCK. IT WAS KARMA.
BUT STILL, WE LOVED OUR TEAM
AND NOW THEY'VE PAID US BACK WITH THIS GREAT VICTORY

SO MUCH FOR THE CURSE OF THE BAMBINO
IT TURNS OUT THAT THE BABE WAS NOT TO BLAME
THE BOSTON RED SOX ARE NOW BASEBALL'S CHAMPIONS
AND THE FEELINGS FOR OUR TEAM ARE NOT THE SAME.
    (END)

(One by one, Rooters take off their raccoon coats and hang them on the coat rack. Then the Father takes off his coat, and with a smile, he places his coat there, as well. He joins the Rooters front and center.)

                                        ALL
There's always THIS year!

                            BLACKOUT

                            CURTAIN

A Little Business,
A Little Ballgame

ELIZABETH PARISEAU

As always when Sheila awoke, it was cold. Didn't matter the season — the very early morning always had a chill.

Didn't matter the number of four a.m.s she saw, either; waking up was always hard. Her mouth and eyes were dry. The soles of her feet reacted with shock against the chilly floors.

Did it matter that her apartment was a tiny dump? No carpets and the floors weren't even wood but ratty linoleum, in some places worn through enough to expose yet another layer of linoleum beneath, in strange little pools of conflicting patterns like mineral stains. But was it important, when she only ever saw it at the ugly ends of each day, and both times through half-shut eyes?

She put the kettle on, as she did every morning. As she did every morning, she selected a bag of Earl Grey from the box on the counter. She hated her own habit of picking the best teabags first, so that by the end of each week, when getting up was that much harder, only the crappier bags would be left.

And yet the habit never changed.

As with every morning, she was still on the toilet when the kettle shrieked. She listened to it for a few seconds, unwilling to get up again just yet, content to doze and listen to it howl. It was one of the small contentments, she thought, of being so totally alone — there was no husband or even a cat to panic with the teapot's shrieking, and the other rathole apartments above and below her had stood vacant since September.

I live in a vacuum, she thought. *A vacuum with linoleum floors.*

Sheila returned to the kitchen and stifled the kettle, poured the steaming water into the stained brown mug, and dipped the bag till it thickened into tea. The warmth of the liquid filled her stomach falsely, at least for a little while. The tea was breakfast; she would tuck a Nutri-Grain bar into her pocket for later, when she'd be able to eat without gagging. She had never been able to take solid food right away.

Outside, the cold was stinging. She revved the engine on the Oldsmobile. It was dun colored and wide-bodied, in both of those ways like an old war horse. It never started without complaint, which Sheila enjoyed, as she rarely did either.

She drove the rattling Olds through streets empty save for the other "grunts," the blue collar workers, some of whom found waking with the dawn a point of pride, and all of whom found it a necessity. The bum on the corner was bundled as best he could against the 15-degree New England weather; his breath stood out in the cold.

She pulled into the parking lot of Palm Manor Nursing Home at 4:56 a.m., as she did every morning; she was never later or earlier for the 5 a.m. start of her shift.

Working with the elderly was not as intensive a manual labor as, say, jackhammer operation, but it wore on you in other ways. There was a sense of manning the end of the line. It was only a quasi-medical facility — full of tubes and rubber and the ineradicable smell of urine, but none of the equipment was designed for resuscitation or cure. It all amounted to a kind of waiting room, a layover. Her job was to stamp everyone's passport, smile, and offer a complimentary beverage. And wipe their asses, if need be.

Inside, the air was hot and scratchy, like trying to breathe raw wool. Didn't matter the season — the nursing home was always stifling. The air was always close. She stripped off her scarf and coat hurriedly, leaving on the pink scrubs with the wide pockets, a laminated name tag hanging from her hip. As she hung up her coat, already Mischa was yelling.

George Ressner did not know where he was. And yet, the not knowing was familiar.

He examined the room carefully, suddenly feeling a memory come across with a searing flash, of a book he had read with his grandchildren, a book where Winnie the Pooh and friends pick up pebbles and put them in a sock, a sock which turns out to have a hole, and the pebbles fall out, one by one. *Piglet looked into the sock and counted very carefully...*

Grandchildren.

He turned his head slowly toward the window, where the mauve curtains held back the first light of the morning. Or perhaps the last light of dusk. There was no way to tell.

Grandchildren.

Well, yes. He looked down at his hands. They were papery and wrinkled and liver-spotted and they shook when he picked them up off the bed. The right hand in particular seemed as if it were made of wood. He brought his left hand toward it and began to pry at the paralyzed fingers, massage flexibility into the dead hand. He did not know why it was that way. He did not know he spent his every waking moment massaging that unresponsive right hand with the left.

He did not know where he was.

It was tempting, he thought, to cry about that. To scream. To demand an explanation. But as he grew more aware of his body, he sensed he was at least well cared for. For the time being, knowing just that would have to do.

Soon after having that thought, he felt a spreading wetness in his pajamas. He yanked at the covers, but the smell answered his question before his eyes did. He replaced the blankets over his lap and looked at the window again. It was either very early or very late. He couldn't tell which.

"Mr. Ressner, good morning." Sheila chirped it as cheerfully as she could, breezing into his room and throwing back the curtain.

Soon she would be stripping off his urine-soaked pajama bottoms, as she did every morning without fail. She had long since given up on getting to Mr. Ressner before he wet himself — instead her method was to check him frequently, changing him whenever he'd had an "accident." He was virtually guaranteed to have wet the bed first thing in the morning, and trying to make him wear diapers had touched off a tantrum. More than a tantrum. The diapers had made him wander the halls when he should have been asleep. Made him venture into other rooms. The diapers had made him keep the whole ward awake with his yelling at night. Far better to compromise with a daily changing, Sheila thought, or such had been her "executive decision," as she called it. Mischa would have reprimanded them both if she knew, and she could easily have known, but seemed to prefer not to; the peace and quiet was apparently worth it to her, too. Sheila held up her end of the bargain by checking Mr. Ressner first thing, even if Goldie was already crying in her room across the hall.

"Did Ted come by last night?" she asked as she sat him, newly dressed, gently down in a chair so she could change the bed.

He stopped his bewildered examinations of the chair long enough to look up at her and demand, "Who the hell is Ted?"

Sheila said nothing, continuing to strip the sheets. Ever so slightly, she shook her head. Today was going to be one of Mr. Ressner's bad days.

Of course, it was Murphy's law, she thought to herself with a grim little smile. His asshole son was coming for his biannual visit today; why not give him a show?

Sheila couldn't be sure if Mr. Ressner had real Alzheimer's or not. She knew it was the formal diagnosis on his charts, would probably be listed as his cause of death. She supposed that every brain was different.

But she knew that there was only so much variation — otherwise, in her line of work, things had a theme, an underlying progression that never varied. Alzheimer's patients might hang at the edge of phases — one day, while on the verge of losing a skill, they might seem as if it had never been threatened; then, the next it might seem as if they'd never tied their shoes before; then, three days later, they'd slap your hands away in bewilderment when you reached for the laces. But once the transitional phase was over, there was no more returning to the previous stage. Once the shoelaces had lain useless for a few weeks, it was over — no going back.

But Mr. Ressner... while otherwise his disease progressed normally, eating away at first his mind and then his body in its inexorable pattern, one strange phenomenon seemed temporarily to change its course — the visits from Ted.

That's what he called him, just "Ted."

Once long ago, he'd told Sheila out of nowhere that he'd had a visitor. Thinking it was his son, but playing along, Sheila had asked who.

"Ted," he'd said, with a little smirk.

That first time, and for a few times after that, Sheila had let it go. But finally, she'd asked, "Ted who?"

He'd leaned close to her and whispered, like quoting a litany, "The Splendid Splinter. Number Nine. The Great Ted Williams."

"Are you a big baseball fan, Mr. Ressner?" she'd asked, trying to sound jovial. She already knew he wasn't, or if he was, he never showed it — most people in this area were baseball mad, and many of the patients in the home kept up with the sports sections or at least had ball-caps with those red "B"s on them. But not George. His walls were bare. She never even saw him watch a baseball game.

Frankly, it gave Sheila the creeps.

And there was more. Mr. Ressner had no actual visitors save his son, and the things he said about Ted never followed one of those visits. Nor did they follow visits from the doctor — Ted only came at night.

And while she often found him wet first thing in the morning and at least twice a day, he never seemed to have accidents during the night. And when Ted came, he wouldn't the next day, either.

In fact, most perplexingly, Ted's visits seemed to somehow reverse the course of Mr. Ressner's Alzheimer's disease, if only temporarily; for the next day or so, he'd be continent and 100 percent more coherent. His recoveries, moreover, would last only as long as visits from Ted did; Sheila had learned to immediately recognize the signs. Mr. Ressner's eyes would twinkle. He would recognize her — he hardly ever remembered her name, but after a visit from Ted, he wouldn't look at her as if starting from scratch. Where on his bad days Mr. Ressner would grunt out short, hostile answers, after visits from Ted he'd carry on a polite, even cheerful conversation.

He would acknowledge Ted had visited, but he never brought it up himself. And he would never tell anyone what he and Ted spoke about.

"Oh," he'd say mischievously, looking askance. "A little business. A little ballgame."

It was all he'd ever say. "A little business, a little ballgame."

It was far from rude — in fact, it was charming. Sheila even thought, in these post-Ted conversations, that she could see the man Mr. Ressner had once been. And she almost wished she couldn't. Because when Ted stopped coming — and he always eventually stopped coming — Mr. Ressner would be back to square one. The confusion. The helplessness. The anger. Sheila couldn't decide whether Ted was a curse or a blessing — Mr. Ressner's recoveries were miraculous, but every time he'd relapse, he'd get just a little worse.

The visit from Robert Ressner went as poorly as Sheila expected.

"Right this way, Mr. Ressner," Mischa crowed, jostling along noiselessly in her white shoes over the gleaming hallway floor.

George's son grunted and followed her, his black wingtips letting out the occasional squeal.

Kissass, Sheila thought, following behind them both, narrowing her eyes at Mischa's back.

Robert Ressner, only child of George and the late Gloria Ressner, was an imposing man, well over six feet, with an athletic build and a full, bushy head of hair, though he neared 60. Mischa thought he looked like John F. Kennedy Jr., and, mortifyingly, had told him so. Sheila thought he looked more like Jay Leno, and kept that to herself.

Sheila assumed Mischa, her brain affected by the endless chain of bodice-rippers she read on her meal breaks, fantasized about being swept off her feet by Robert Ressner — she was atwitter for several days before his visits to the home, and fussed constantly about the appearance of the ward and George Ressner's room and, of course, George Ressner's behavior, sticking her nose into everything Sheila did, making it almost impossible for Sheila to get anything done, or, for that matter, to avoid giving Mischa — with whom her supervisor-employee relationship was strained at the best of times — a hearty slap in the face and spirited lecture on being realistic about her chances with the CEOs of Fortune 500 Companies who were only ever in her presence while visiting their senile fathers, and even then only out of guilt and a sense of obligation —

Robert Ressner had stopped suddenly in the doorway to his father's room. Sheila very nearly ran into him, caught up as she was in her hateful thoughts about Mischa.

Robert Ressner had been the architect of several hostile industry takeovers and a few bankruptcies and collapsed venture capital schemes. Like a battle-hardened general, he was not one to betray surprise or consternation. So he just stood there, mouth slightly open, blinking at his father in bed, watching the PGA Tour on his wall-mounted television.

George Ressner sat upright in his hospital bed. His sweatsuit — picked out special by Mischa for the occasion — was in a puddle on the floor next to him. George Ressner was stark naked, and looking all of his 87 years.

Robert swallowed, still saying nothing.

Mischa glowered at Sheila.

Sure, throw me *under the bus,* Sheila thought, narrowing her eyes right back.

George never looked down from the golf match.

Robert muttered something about coming back another time, turned on his heel, and retreated out the door and down the hallway. At his heels went Mischa, babbling excuses and apologies.

Still in the room, Sheila looked at George and sighed. But for his nakedness, he was perfectly normal-looking, calm, content and well-behaved. *Just the same,* she thought, *I had best have him clothed before Mischa sees him again.*

Sheila approached the bed, letting out a groan as she bent to scoop up the clothes off the floor. She stuffed them in the plastic-lined hamper in the corner, went to his closet and found a new set of pajamas for him to wear.

He still hadn't budged when she approached the bed again. She put a hand on his arm, on his thin, papery skin, and he jumped, looking at her with wide eyes of alarm and incomprehension.

After dressing George, who stepped back into his pajamas without complaint, Sheila left the room, closing the door softly behind her. She walked quietly but briskly a few feet down the hall to the supply closet, shutting herself in.

Then she laughed until the tears rolled down her face.

Later that night, she visited the library for the first time in at least ten years, if not the first time since she graduated high school.

Even later, she fell asleep on the couch, a Ted Williams biography open on her lap. Next to her were more books on Williams, a few on baseball and the Red Sox in general, and one called *On Death and Dying*.

She didn't know why, but she was moved and fascinated by George. She knew next to nothing about baseball beyond the occasional reports on the news or conversations overheard at the grocery store or gas station. Everyone around here was a baseball savant, like they'd all drunk the same tainted water as a kid, and sometimes she felt like the only normal one left, the only one who'd been immune.

But the concept of Ted and George wasn't about the game — that she could sense. She supposed Mr. Ressner was actually old enough to have really known Ted Williams, for the great ballplayer to have been his friend. Stranger things, after all, had happened, and patients with dementia often became confused, shuttling in and out of time, thinking a daughter was a wife or a son an old army pal. She supposed it was also possible that a man with no previously expressed love for baseball or the Red Sox to hallucinate visits from Ted Williams as well, but her armchair psychologist's research and experience with people at the end of their lives told her Ted was George's way of transitioning somehow — his own concept of the Angel of Death. She'd even seen something like it before, especially in patients with senile dementia, who would see a long-dead relative or friend. Someone who appeared to them like a guide, a heavenly welcoming committee. One woman had actually seen her dearly departed cat.

But none of them had seen a celebrity, at least not that Sheila remembered. And more importantly, none had ever showed the regaining of their faculties the way George did. This was what made George her golden opportunity — he could go in and out of his fugue state; he was the only patient Sheila had yet encountered who could not only experience full-on dementia, but also come back and talk to her about it. She wanted to know how. She wanted to know what he talked about with Ted. She wanted, in short, a sneak peek at what it was really like to die — the spiritual part, rather than the physical indignities. More than that, she wanted to know the point of it all, the moral to this Aesop fable.

She found herself obsessed, suddenly, in the weeks following Robert Ressner's visit, with the need to find out, before George, too, had passed on. It felt like some festering existential crisis she hadn't known was brewing had come to a head, and it all centered on George. She became possessive of him, and, though she didn't want to admit it, she began to show him favoritism. She watched him as much as she could for signs Ted had returned. Otherwise, she prepared, and thought, and waited.

Several weeks later, the day finally came — just when she had begun to believe it wouldn't.

After the incident with Robert, George had deteriorated sharply. She could no longer keep up with his changings — Mischa had found her out and ordered that he be in diapers at all times. The return of the diapers meant the return of tantrums, only these tantrums went further, sometimes landing George in restraints for the night. He lost the ability to communicate verbally and recognized no one, yet babbled nonsense to his own image in the mirror. He chewed on things like a baby, wanting to put everything in his mouth. He grunted, groaned, and screamed wordlessly when awake. Mercifully, though, he slept much more in this latest terrible descent into the abyss — often fifteen hours a day or more. Sheila worried that she'd missed her opportunity.

And then one morning, after a particularly bad spell, she found George awake, dry and lucid, though still in the restraints.

"What the hell are these things?" was the first thing he said, tugging on them.

"They're..." she started, still recovering from the surprise of him speaking clearly.

"Handcuffs," he said as she reached to untie them. "That the kind of joint you're running?"

"You're not...aware of it, Mr. Ressner," she stammered, unbuckling the padded cuff from around his left wrist and placing it gently in his lap, willing her hands to stop shaking. "But you've been having problems behaving lately, and—"

"So he was right," George said, laying his head back on his pillow and sounding defeated.

Sheila had moved to the right cuff now, but she stopped. There were a million things to say, to ask. She glanced at the door — Mischa would have a fit if she caught Sheila unbuckling George by herself, and she certainly wouldn't be placated by a story about the ghost of Ted Williams visiting in the night.

Seeing no one coming, she began working on the second buckle, and said softly, "George."

He looked at her.

"What...what does Ted look like?" she asked, her voice shaking. The questions she'd saved up wanted to come out in a rush, the bluntest and most audacious first.

"Hmm, oh, he's a pretty tall lanky fella, I guess," George said, shrugging.

Sheila tried again. "Is he old, or young?"

"Dunno, he said. "Little older than me, I think."

That told her nothing — she had no idea how old George thought he was.

"Are you friends?" she asked.

"Well, sure," he answered. "He visits me, don't he?"

"Right," she nodded encouragingly. "So did you know him, when he was playing baseball?"

"Well, of course!" he said. "Who didn't?"

She stifled a sigh of exasperation. "How did you meet him?" she asked.

"Why are you askin' so many questions?" he asked back, peering at her with narrowed eyes. "You best mind your business, Missy."

"But," she said, leaning closer. "But I just want to know why he visits you."

"Dunno," George said, looking at the drawn curtains in front of the window. "Lonely guy, maybe."

"You said he was right about something," she tried. "What was he right about?"

"Can you open that window curtain there, dear?" he said. "Be nice to have some scenery to look at."

By the time she turned back from the window, he was asleep again.

She tried him again later (the young visiting doctor was pleased when he made the rounds that morning, thinking George's improvement was the result of an experimental drug he had prescribed).

But George still stuck to that answer — "a little business, a little ballgame," when she asked directly about their conversations. He'd give shrugging, non-committal answers to her more general questions as he had in the morning — and when the questions had gone on for any length of time, he'd interrupt to ask for a drink of water or to move the window shade or to take him to the bathroom, and the conversation would be over.

When she left work that day, it was dark again — still the dead of winter, the doldrums of February, just at the point where it seems spring will never come. The sun going down had plunged the temperature another ten degrees, making the parking lot and the path to her car slick with black ice.

The Oldsmobile's engine coughed indignantly when she first turned the key.

"Piece of shit," she muttered, trying it again. She felt her first urge for a cigarette in more than two years; she hadn't smoked in five.

Another cough. Then nothing.

She slumped back in her seat, looking out the window and chewing absentmindedly on one fingernail until her breath inside the chilly car fogged the window up. And then she sat there some more, not looking at anything. Thinking.

Ted never came back after that.

The day George died, it was early April. It was overcast, occasionally spitting a weak drizzle, and then finally darkening to deep thunder-heads and driving downpours as medical orderlies arrived to prepare his body for transport to the morgue.

He'd died in the early hours of the morning. The nurse on the shift before hers had found him. Sheila was disappointed by this, felt jealous. George had become *hers* somehow — it was deeply unfair she'd missed his last moments, missed even being the first to know he was gone.

She busied herself cleaning out his possessions from the drawers and cabinets, listening to the orderlies bitch about the Sox game being rained out. Apparently, they'd had bleacher seats.

She began with his nightstand, first putting his bottles of lotion and medicated ointment and a framed photograph of his wife into a plastic bag labeled "PATIENT'S POSSESSIONS."

On a shelf at the bottom were some old issues of *National Geographic*, his reading glasses, an empty hot water bottle. The drawer of the night-stand was empty.

Well, almost empty.

She could barely keep her composure after opening that drawer, sweeping a hand around the back of it, and feeling the one solid object inside.

Before she could stop and think, she had pocketed it. She spent the rest of her shift patting it through her wide uniform pocket, making sure it was still there, in fear that someone would spot the bulge through her clothing. In fear the son knew about it, would come looking for it — but wouldn't he already have taken it if that were so?

Already she was getting carried away, try as she might to simply finish her shift without attracting notice. She trembled with excitement as she changed sheets. She grinned through bedpans. She smiled a bit too wide at Goldie, and Goldie started to cry.

Outside in the car again she tried to tell herself not to jump the gun. It could be a fake. She'd need to do some research. And what if there was something else she'd missed? She knew it was unlikely, that she'd scoured the room removing George's possessions. But still! What if . . . ?

Taking it out again, she felt a sense of peace wash over her. Yes, this was the real thing. Yes, and if there had been something else in that room, it hadn't been meant for her. How else to explain the way it'd been hidden in plain sight, where even the most perfunctory snooping would have uncovered it? What were the odds of it still even being there for her to find when she did?

Warm from her pocket, the baseball sat perfectly nestled in her hand. It was worn and scuffed, its red stitches faded, the way you'd expect an old baseball to be.

Written on it in ink, in a sharp script, was the inscription —
Thanks for everything
Ted Williams

The Tragedie of Theo (Prince of Red Sox Nation)

STEVE ALMOND

DRAMATIS PERSONAE:

Theo, Prince of Red Sox Nation
Lucchino, King of Red Sox Nation
Shaughlonius, a Wicked Scribe
Rosencrantz & Adamstern, Theo's minions
Ghost, an Apparition

Act I
SETTING: *The royal court of Red Sox Nation*

LUCCHINO:
Young Theo, cast thy nighted colour off
And let thine eye fall on joyous Yawkey!
Though our side bow'd to the palest Sox
Still the nation bathes in the glory of 04.
And we shall reign again if by signature
You will affirm this generous pledge
(*Lucchino produces a thick folio, in triplicate, and sets it before Theo with a flourish*)

THEO:
Let me mull the matter, wise Lucchino

LUCCHINO:
Come now, dear prince! Mulling tis dulling!
Our fevered legions await your fickle pen

THEO *(inspecting the folio with knitted brow)*:
I merely ask a faire compensation
and a few hush'd hours contemplation

Act II

SETTING: *A Dark Corner of Ye Olde Cask & Flagon*

SHAUGHLONIUS:
Why the somber mien, my liege?

LUCCHINO:
Theo.

SHAUGHLONIUS:
The Crown Prince? But he is like kin to you.

LUCCHINO:
Aye, kin he is and less than kind.

SHAUGHLONIUS:
How so, my liege?

LUCCHINO:
I offer him a king's ransom and he scoffs!
He is young and starv'd of glory's fruit
Upon which he gorges while I play villain!
I, who plucked the lad green from obscurity
And made him a prince among players!
(Lucchino slams back a draught of whiskey)

SHAUGHLONIUS:
Oh, callow youth! Hath he no gratitude for his patron?
Perhaps 'twere best the fans learned the truth?

LUCCHINO:
Very well, I shall summon the Herald!

SHAUGHLONIUS:
Nay! Methinks the Globe a better means by half.
Pray now, noble king, simply tell your tale...

Act III

SETTING: *A rampart high atop the Greene Monster*

THEO:
To sign, or not to sign, that is the question:
Whether 'tis nobler to suffer the slings
and Ordways of outrageous publick relations,
the whining hopes of an aggrieved peoples,
or by scotching the deal win some sleep!
But sleep — perchance to dream. Ay, there's the rub!
For what if I should dream of scarlet stockings
rounding third and vanquished Yankees?
As night fog hangs upon the Greene Monster
so too is my heart a doubtful shroud.

Enter Rosencrantz & Adamstern, out of breath and brandishing a
broadsheet

ROSENCRANTZ:
Alack, there he is!

ADAMSTERN:
Prince Theo!

THEO:
What eager tidings bring ye trusted minions?

ROSENCRANTZ:
See here, gentle Prince! A proclamation —

ADAMSTERN:
Writ by Shaughlonius, whose poison pen —

ROSENCRANTZ:
Proclaims you an ingrate swelled on praises —

ADAMSTERN:
Deserving of our duplicitous king, Lucchino!

Theo reads the broadsheet with a look of growing horror; it drops
from his hands

Act IV
SETTING: *A graveyard off Landsdowne Street; Prince Theo, backlit by the
sodium lights of Fenway Park, is seen holding a skull aloft*

THEO:
Alas, poor Ducette, I knew him well.

The Ghost appears; he is a stout figure who hovers, half seen, in
shadow. Startled, Prince Theo drops the skull.

THEO:
Who goes there?

GHOST:
A friend from the fields beyond, rest assured.

THEO:
Would that I could rest at all.

GHOST:
Why should our lord be mired in such despair?

Theo pulls the folded broadsheet from his pocket and hands it to the
Ghost

THEO:
Have I not toil'd to honor my home towne team?
Would the king mop credit from my brow?

For it was I who claimed the mighty Papi!
A fortune for Foulke, a killing for Schilling!
Was I not the man who slay'd our long shame?

GHOST:
Aye, 'tis betrayal that wounds deepest.
But a Prince must be his own man, lest he
never be a king in his own kingdom.

THEO:
Shall I abandon the soil of my birth, then,
the farm system I seeded, my beloved Fen?
And leave to Lucchino the harvest to come?

GHOST:
Fear not, young lord. The king and his kind
Shall suffer dearly when you depart.
The fans, now revolted, will revolt
And the winning ways will quickly halt!
As for you, a new legacy awaits to the West
While a curse of 86 years comes here to rest.

THEO:
Would that it were so, strange spirit.

The Ghost steps from the shadows to reveal a broad, familiar face. He holds a bat in one hand and takes a savage swing. Suddenly, a ball is flying through the air. It strikes the sodium lights above Fenway Park, which explode all into darkness.

GHOST:
Fear not, gentle Prince. I know curses.

THE END

The Sixth Game

DAVID DESJARDINS

Al Nipper is on the mound against the Yankees on an August afternoon so foggy they have put on the lights at Fenway. The mist
droops over the tall green wall in left field and already the Yankees have
misplayed two routine fly balls. My friend Willie, a New York fan, is not
pleased.

Nipper is a mediocre pitcher, a junkballer who after four years in the
majors has lost as many games as he has won, but for some reason he has
always baffled the Yankee hitters. That is why I have brought Willie to
Fenway today: to gloat after Nipper confounds them again. Willie knows
that, but he has come anyway. Red Sox fans, he says, should not be
denied small pleasures, because they will never enjoy great ones.

He is referring, of course, to my team's embarrassing record in the
68 years since 1918. It being a characteristic of Yankees and Red Sox fans
to despise each others' teams as much as they love their own, Willie
knows that record well, and reminds me of it often. True, he did send me
a sincere note of condolence after Boston's humiliating defeat in the
sixth game of last year's World Series. But he continues to believe that
the Sox are so illustrious at losing simply because they and their fans,
deep in their hearts, love it.

I see her in the fourth inning. On a hit-and-run play, Wade Boggs
pokes a liner down the third-base line. As Ellis Burks sprints around
second, I lose track of the ball as it bounds out of sight into the corner,
but see Loretta leaning forward from her box seat, watching the play in
left field, her hands tightened into fists. The crowd roar mounts and
Loretta's eyes dart about, and I know that the Yankee left-fielder can't
get a handle on the ball and there'll be a play at the plate. As Loretta

turns to watch the wide arc of the throw and see Burks slide in safely, she jumps, her fists in the air and her long ponytail bobbing against her back. She brings one arm down around the neck of the man next to her, and he pulls her by the waist to him. Sox lead, 1—0.

I nudge Willie with my elbow and he shrugs — not to worry, the game is young. Has he intentionally misinterpreted my gesture, or has he not spotted her? I can't tell.

Loretta is the only woman I know who understands the infield fly rule, has strong opinions about the designated hitter, and plans March vacations in Winter Haven. I still love her.

Mike Greenwell flies out and Boggs is left stranded at second. Between innings, people file past our seats to buy beer. Loretta's boyfriend is one of them. As he passes, he chats with a young boy in front of him. He is gregarious and confident. I understand why Loretta likes him.

Nipper finishes his warmups, the infielders toss the ball around, and Don Mattingly steps to the plate. He is perhaps the best hitter in the majors, and Willie straightens in his seat in anticipation. But Nipper is scrappy. He has no fast ball, certainly nothing Mattingly can't get around on, but his junk is hopping: a sweeping curve and a knuckle-ball bobbing like a bumblebee as it moves to the plate. Mattingly grounds out weakly to first.

"Just not their day," I say, as musically as I can. No one has ever called me a good winner. "Right, uh huh," Willie grunts. Nipper is inex-plicable to Willie, a freak of nature the Yanks should have knocked out in the first inning. When the next two hitters go down just as easily, I punch my knee. I look to the box seats and see that Loretta is doing the same.

We met last October at Brooksie's Tavern, the night of the sixth game. I was there with some guys from work, as I had been for each of the pre-vious five. When the Sox went ahead 3—2 in the seventh, I bought a round of beers for the table of boisterous women behind us, and Loretta, among them, invited me over. I was taken by her long reddish brown hair, her dark eyes, her keen sense of the rhythms of the game. She told me that her three brothers had each been lights-out pitchers for Central years back and that they went in together on a pair of Red Sox season tickets. She took the cap off my head, put it on hers, and wrote her phone number on back of the scorecard I was keeping.

Three innings later, as the last ground ball trickled under Bill Buckner's legs and the jubilant Mets poured onto the field, I took my beer and my sour stomach to a table at the back of the bar. Only minutes before, the Sox, on the strength of a sublime home run by Dave Henderson, had been one strike away from winning it all, the Shea Stadium scoreboard flashing "Congratulations Boston Red Sox 1986 World Champs." Now this.

The bar emptied quickly, and Loretta walked over and sat beside me. From our booth, we watched the wide-screen TV in silence like two players in a dugout. Loretta took my hand and said, "Just remember, it will never be worse than this."

I looked at her, dazed and a little drunk. My chest was thick with despair. I tried to speak, but couldn't. She said, "No, really, just breathe. Keep breathing." She took the beer from my hand, put it on the table, and sat with me quietly, like she might have done with a friend at a wake. Later she led me out of Brooksie's and took me home.

I know there are those who will say our romance was doomed from the start, having been born in a moment of such desolation. Two days later, we took to my bed with a bottle of whisky to watch the seventh game on TV, more from a sense of duty than from expectation, or even hope, that the Sox would rebound. That night we made love in an alcohol-sweetened affirmation of something other than the fortunes of the players whose images flickered on the screen behind us.

Maybe it was because the reversal the Sox suffered in the sixth game was so extreme, so cruel, but something changed in the world last fall. The off-season was illogically full of lightness. Loretta and I waded into the waning days of 1986 without a thought of baseball or the sixth game or the spring. We were new and whole again.

She began taking me to basketball games — an inferior sport, I admit. Loretta is not very discriminating in her passions. But it didn't matter. I cheered when she cheered, booed when she booed, and was happy to do so. Something in me seemed to unclench. The rigorous inner discipline of the Sox fan — the policing of body posture and attitude that mystically communicates support to the team — melted away with the winter. The world began to relax all around us.

I introduced her to Willie. We met him at Leo's pub, and I stepped back from the bar and let them talk, like a scout showing off a prospect who has the stuff to make it to the bigs. Willie was impressed, and despite her being a Sox fan, he too fell in love with Loretta. I was very happy.

As Opening Day approached, eagerness and wariness mixed in the spring air. We both wondered: Could the Sox recover from the trauma of the sixth game? The reports from Winter Haven were not encouraging — shoddy defense, weak offense. Still, I told Loretta, with a starting rotation so strong, even Don Zimmer could win a pennant.

We managed a couple of bleacher seats from a scalper for the home opener, a glorious game in which Bruce Hurst humbled the Blue Jays, shutting them out on two hits. So heightened was our glee that, driving home afterward, we had to pull into a Holiday Inn off Route 9, take a room, and make celebratory love. I felt giddy. The trees brushing our window were the lush green of April, but to us it seemed October, the season of champions. I like to remember us like that — lying there, flushed and sleepy with victory, confident of our stuff as the future lay in front of us like cool, moist outfield grass before a game.

But then Oil Can Boyd developed a mysterious knot in his throwing arm and Roger Clemens faltered after a bitter contract dispute. Soon the Sox were out of the pennant race almost before it had begun.

I did not deal well with these disappointments. I became impatient with friends, and especially with Loretta. We had arguments before, of course, but this was different. Now I began to handle even small disagreements poorly. One day I stood her up on a date to attend a family picnic, in order to stay home and watch the Sox play — of all teams — the lowly Orioles.

Willie tried to talk some sense to me: What is this ridiculous ball-club compared to what you have with Loretta? What's with this self-destructive behavior? In truth, considering his opinion of Sox fans, I think he wasn't surprised that I would bobble such an easy roller. But to me it was a matter of reflexes, and I felt powerless to change the situation.

Finally, after a few weeks of dates characterized by long periods of silence, Loretta wanted out. I did not argue the call.

When I was nine, my father took my brother and me to Fenway to see Dave Morehead pitch against the Indians. It was the day of his no-hitter, a rare moment of glory. In the late innings, I focused every bit of mental energy I had toward willing Morehead to success. My brother, perverse as usual, rooted for the Indians to tie the game up and send it to extra innings so we wouldn't have to go home. But my father was not a rooter — to him only the game mattered, and the moments of grace and beauty it revealed, regardless of which team performed them. He watched the game in neither hope nor despair. My father was, I think, a happy man. Of all the things I inherited from him, happiness was not one of them.

Watching Loretta from my seat beside Willie, I feel what countless Boston players must have felt over the past 68 years: the insult of what could have been. Loretta's boyfriend has long blond hair, height, and an easy smile. He says something to Loretta and she laughs. I am shorter, with dark curly hair, and by common consensus, a bit too serious. It occurs to me that maybe I just didn't make her laugh enough.

It will never be worse than this. Breathe, just breathe.

Another of the new kids up from Pawtucket, Todd Benzinger, steps to the plate. The rookies have been the sole positive note in a disappointing season for the Sox. It is a rebuilding year for the team, and Benzinger has great promise. On the first pitch, he hits a shot off the left-field wall so hard and fast he has to settle for a single. He stands easily on the bag and chats with Mattingly at first base. He is too young to hate the Yankees.

Benzinger takes a long lead off first, too long for my liking. Ron Guidry, the Yankee pitcher, has a worrisome move to first base; he is masterful at picking off runners. Benzinger should know this, of course, but still I yell for him to get back. He can't hear; he is a character in a movie. Beside me, Willie leans forward, his right leg fidgeting rapidly.

Guidry studiously ignores Benzinger. He bobs the rosin bag in his hand; he stares abstractedly into center field, rubbing the ball with both hands. He turns to the plate, glove hand on one knee, shakes off a sign from the catcher, then nods and straightens. He has not once looked over to first.

My stomach tightens; how can Benzinger not see the danger of his situation?

In one humiliatingly graceful move, Guidry whirls and throws hard and low, and Mattingly tags Benzinger sliding head-first back to the bag. The rookie, head down, walks slowly back to the dugout as the Fenway crowd boos.

I have thought long and hard about the question of evil in the world. Why do good things come to grief? In Willie's view, human beings are the sole agents of their own undoing. Thus he argues, the massive shift of power from the Red Sox to the Yankees over the course of this century was not the work of spiritual beings, but of one man — the vile Harry Frazee, the Red Sox owner who in a money-hungry frenzy sold Babe Ruth and other stars to the Yankees, engineering a talent drain from which the Sox have never recovered.

Still, I challenge Willie — or anyone — to explain the sixth game to me. I am not a religious man, but I know in my soul that there were unearthly forces moving about the world that night that took the victory from the Sox and handed it to the undeserving Mets. Damn them. Damn them all. Why didn't McNamara leave Clemens in to finish off the Mets? Why didn't he pull the gimpy-kneed Buckner in the 10th for a defensive replacement? And tell me this, Willie, you smug son of a bitch, why, damn it, is she not sitting here with me now?

I look at Willie sitting there, sipping his beer, his heart untroubled, his world in order, his mind on the game.

To hell with the game. I have had enough of the game. The game is a cheat and a lie. I look to Loretta and, by power of will, summon her from her seat. She rises, edges past the people in her row, and walks up toward me.

As she passes my row, I put my beer down and follow her past the highest tier of seats. She walks by a concession stand, and as I follow, women pull their boyfriends from my path; I am a dangerous man.

Loretta stops behind the seats high above home plate, watching the game through the iron mesh net which hangs from the roof of Fenway. I walk up next to her and lean against the seats, my back to the field. Loretta watches me quietly. My angry face amuses her.

She turns back to the game. "I knew you'd be here today, with the Nip pitching," she says. "Willie too?"

"Yeah."

Loretta nods thoughtfully. She is quiet, then tugs my hand. "Look."

"I don't want to," I say, but I do and Loretta knows it. She twists me around and we both watch as Sam Horn steps to the plate. He is a bull of a man, and as he slowly paws the ground in the batter's box and taps his bat, we wait reverently.

Guidry comes in tight with the first one, and the crowd boos at the brushback. "I miss you too, you know," Loretta says, squeezing my hand. I shake my head. Not now. You have made me watch the game, so be quiet. Guidry's next pitch is inviting, low and on the corner, but Horn holds back. The count is 2 and 0. I lean toward Loretta. "This next one. You watch."

Horn steps lazily back into the box and Guidry winds and delivers a slow curve that Horn crushes so hard the Yankee outfielders just turn and watch it land deep into the center field bleachers. "Jesus," Loretta and I both whisper as the crowd stands and applauds.

We watch Horn round the bases and tip his cap to the fans on his way to the dugout. "It looks good for next year, with all these kids," Loretta says. "Don't you think?"

"Yes, I do."

"Of course, the bullpen needs some help."

"Of course."

She is quiet a moment. "It wouldn't have worked out, you know that?"

"I know."

We watch Spike Owen step to the plate. Loretta pulls her purse back up around her shoulder. "Well, I have to get back to my seat."

"I know." I wait a moment. "So I'll call you, right?"

Loretta looks at me and shakes her head, as if I never cease to amaze her, but we both know that isn't true — I ceased to amaze her some time ago. Still, she takes a deep breath and says, "Yes, call me."

She lets go of my hand and walks off. As she leaves, she turns and yells to me, "Tell Willie the Yankees suck."

"I will."

Owen grounds out and the Sox are retired. I walk back to the third-base side of the park and descend to my seat. My beer is where I left it, and I drink, watching the Sox outfielders toss the ball around. The fog seems to be lifting a bit.

Loretta passes our row, carrying two beers. In her box seat, she hands one of them to her boyfriend. Then she yells something in the direction of home plate, but I can't tell what.

"Willie," I say, resting my beer on the seat between my legs. Willie turns to me and I watch his face. He's seen Loretta and looks at me a bit sympathetically. "What?"

"The Yankees suck." Willie gives me a disgusted look. "Whatever," he replies, and drinks from his beer and turns back to the game. The Yankees are up.

The Curious Case of
Dr. Belly and Mr. Itcher

MATTHEW HANLON

He lay with his face on the cool, wet infield grass. He was looking at a dewdrop against a canvas of startling green. He felt good, not a care in the world. His stubble-less cheek squashed any number of those same dewdrops into the grass. At first, he'd been feeling the stretch in his neck and twist down his spine as he pressed himself flat on the ground, arms at his sides, glove facing open side up against his left thigh. But as he got deeper into the stretch, and deeper into the grass, he started to see what was in front of him. He drifted off, like the grass was a koan and he a Buddhist monk. He felt at one with everything — the infield, the diamond, the ballpark, the big chunk of land carved out of the Fens, even the Pike and the rest of the expanse of roads spidering away in all directions. He was dew dropped there, in the middle of it all, a seismic event.

Then the baseball ricocheted off the turf, hit his forehead with a hearty *thwack*, and dribbled over to the third base bag.

"Get off the field!" Johnny Pesky didn't look too happy. Actually, Steve wasn't great at reading Johnny, who was waving his left arm and the fungo bat in his right hand. So Steve would have *guessed* he was angry, but after spending a bit of time with Johnny he realized that he got the same way when he was talking about his playing days; his wife, God rest her soul; and the post-game spread. Steve propped himself up on his left arm to see if he got any better idea of which it might be from that vantage point. He could feel the tingle of dewdrops being rubbed out of existence. Johnny scooped another ball off the ground at his feet, tossed it in the air, and cracked it with the bat down the third base line, off Steve's left elbow.

Steve Bellyitcher had an unfortunate name, especially for a pitcher, and especially in this town. He came to Boston the year before, a signing who was not exactly heralded, but neither were people particularly displeased. For the most part, as had happened for the bulk of his career in the big leagues, he was seen as a good number three or four starter, expected to hold down the fort, pitch his share of innings, keep his team in it, and not worry about threatening "fan" mail letters from angry fantasy team owners betting on him (finally) having his breakout year in any number of the acronyms for which he was a cheap pickup, late in the mock draft.

He stood on the third base line massaging his elbow. Actually, he was a lot closer to the third base dugout than the third base line, because Pesky kept shooting him what he thought were dirty looks. His elbow wasn't damaged severely or anything, nor was his head. Heck, he'd taken a harder shot off his head the year before, just about midway through the season. It was no big deal. Happens all the time when you play a sport with a little, white, tightly wound bit of string and cowhide whipping around the field at upwards of 85 miles per hour, and that's just out of the pitcher's hand.

But last year, in a new city, trying to make a new start, getting beaned off the head by a ball coming back probably a *lot* faster than 85 miles per hour and then having a whole season go into the tank, well, *that* hurt, in more ways than one.

People, of course, assumed the shot off the noggin had something to do with his downward spiral. By "people" he meant anyone capable of typing, picking up a phone and dialing a sports radio telephone number, or getting something broadcast. He lost nearly all command he might have had and sent what had been an All-Star caliber season to that point sliding into a very disappointing ending. He'd heard that Boston could be a tough city to play in if you didn't perform. And judging by all the disparaging remarks in the papers about his fragile mental state, the abuse coming from the stands as he warmed up in the bullpen, and the absolutely brutal bloggers picking over his personal appearance, well, he would agree with that statement. For most people. For him, personally, it wasn't the overriding factor in his descent.

When he was a kid pitching in Little League, he had his first encounter with heckling. "We want a pit-cher, not a belly itch-er!" It was in late August, the third inning of his first game ever pitching. He'd been throwing a no-hitter to that point. Not by skill or anything, it was pure luck. He'd never thrown off a mound before, and the team he was pitching against had obviously never heard of plate discipline, so they swung at everything, including the two pitches he threw which hit the umpire. Steve told himself this is why none of those kids ever made it to the bigs.

But the belly itch-er chants started in the top of the third, when he hit the first batter. And he hit him not once but twice. The first time the umpire ruled that the kid had swung at the pitch (which he had), and the second, well, Steve tried to argue that he was swinging again, but didn't win that one. He also hit the next three batters, thereby walking in a run on a total of eight pitches. The next batter following the run hit the one actual strike he threw that day into the pond well beyond the left-field fence. As he rounded the bases the chant started, and poor little seven-year-old Steve just stood out there on the mound, taking it all like a very brave, very short man. It hurt.

He had once asked his dad where their surname came from. He said that it was some ancient and honored position in Merrie Olde Englande, an occupation where one itched both his own belly and the belly of the king to ward off evil spirits. "A very popular and much sought after job," he added. "Our family was legendary." But it didn't help the sting of that one afternoon. Besides, Steve figured his dad was making the whole story up and the truth was he just had a particularly unfortunate name for a pitcher.

One image in particular stood out. She was the mother of Jimmy Piersall, their first baseman and no relation to the big league player. To this point in life, Steve only knew her as an unexceptional woman: pretty, but not too pretty, always wore a brown skirt with a slightly worn hem, and her bright red lipstick stood out on her face like blood on ice cream. On that day she sat in the stands, and as he stood on the mound looking for some sort of relief from the incessant chanting, he saw those lips drawn up and jagged, screaming "belly itch-er" with such venom he imagined the ground sizzled where her spittle landed.

His season continued to slide from there. He finished the year 0 and 3, which was a small miracle in itself, that he was allowed to pitch in two more games. He managed to throw, at a rough guess, seven strikes in around 150 pitches. Thankfully there were no recorded stats in that league.

The next year he got the chance to pitch again. This was due, in large part, to the new town his family found themselves in. Steve's father assured him it wasn't because of his poor pitching performance that they moved, but the thought would never completely leave Steve's mind. The new surroundings agreed with him, because he started four games, winning three of them, and he never once hit an umpire with a pitch. When the opposing team's fans outnumbered his own he heard the occasional 'belly itch-er' heckling, but it never amounted to much more than background noise.

But he still never forgot that day. In fact, on most days he was due to pitch he thought of it. He was convinced that the only thing that could equal that incident...heck, it wasn't an incident, it was a defining epoch, all ten minutes of it. The only thing that could match that day for sheer horror would be a similar set of events happening to him in a major league ballpark. Or, rather, two specific ballparks: Fenway Park and wherever the heck the Philadelphia Phillies were playing these days. But he didn't seriously believe that.

As a much more mature eight-year-old, he thought he had solved the problems with his control of the year before. And it seemed he had, until the summer sun slipped into August, and the day came for Steve to pitch against the Indians of his league.

"It was one bad game, Stevie," his dad said later, poking his head inside the doorjamb of his bedroom. "Don't let it get you down." Steve waved an arm in the air, feeling the full weight of his hand as a dead, limp thing. Then he let it drop to the bed.

But that one game turned into two bad games, then three, then four, until Steve had his brother bruise his right hand with an old hammer that had been lying out in the yard all summer in the rain and sun. His brother, being a bit overzealous, wound up breaking the hand, and Steve missed the rest of the season and basketball season that year.

This would happen again the next year, and the next, and the next. The only difference was that Steve never asked his brother to try and help him out of the season again.

So the abuse he got as a major leaguer in his first season in Boston wasn't that bad, really. He just went out and pitched and got very frustrated when, like every other year, he seemed to run into troubles somewhere around August or so. It was the sudden, inexplicable, annual nosedive that earned him the nickname, amongst ballplayers, and only behind his back, as Dr. Jekyll and Mr. Hyde.

This year would be different, though. And the reason why this year was going to be different was because of his new approach. In the past, being a baseball player, Steve felt obliged to practice certain superstitions. Or at least practice them until whatever he was hoping to influence by practicing them didn't work out like he intended, and then he'd switch to the next one. Last year alone, after being beaned, he tried performing a Kabbalistic ritual before every game he pitched, which failed for the first game, so he took to practicing the ritual, since he'd gone to the trouble of learning the thing, on every game day he *didn't* pitch. Then he tried getting a tattoo. After winning a game and getting a no decision with the tattoo, he lost his next two starts badly. Following the loss, he tried sewing a little piece of a shirt Pedro's midget had left behind onto the inside of his jersey. He was hoping that would atone for the tattoo, and that he wouldn't have to get it removed. Then he shaved his beard into a funny shape. He'd intended it to *not* be funny, originally, but it turned out that way.

They almost worked, too. He was so busy studying whether or not a particular superstition was being effective that he almost didn't notice that he'd pitched a decent game in early September for the first time in 23 years. He didn't get the win, but he only gave up four runs and walked only two in six innings.

This year, after a long, hard talk with his agent and the Sox management, he decided to forgo the superstition altogether and presented Theo with an alternative. Under the terms of this new deal, Steve would draw his usual salary on a bi-weekly basis, pitching every fifth day until the All-Star break. At that juncture he would be paid per start, and, when he "turned," as it said in the contract, and Dave Wallace offered his observational skills as the barometer they'd use to determine at which point that was, Steve would be allowed to offer up his start to one random member of Red Sox Nation attending that day's game, and would take the fan's place in the stands. The fan would pay a nominal fee for the privilege and a souvenir handful of dirt from the mound, Steve's pay for that start would go to the Jimmy Fund, and Steve would have to pay for a full price admission ticket to the game, as well as any beverages or snacks he might have while watching the game.

The PR department was thrilled, as they'd been working on further fan appreciation schemes, and predicted Steve Bellyitcher days would ratchet up the excitement to a level it hadn't seen since Pedro left town.

For once, he was looking forward to August and September. He knew just how to heckle, too, in case things went sour. Maybe he'd even have his brother up to his place for the second half of the season. They'd have plenty of time to hang out, at any rate, maybe play some bocce.

Rain Delay

MICHELLE VON EUW

Her first date is at Fenway Park. She is sixteen and thinks this moment has been a long time coming. All her friends have already been on dates, lots of dates, even the ones who aren't as pretty as she is, the ones with bad skin and bony elbows and split ends.

She isn't sure who she is; but who ever is? Her clothes are standard prep — Gap jeans, polo shirts — but she started streaking her hair last fall. Green streaks during Celtics season, blue when the Pats played, now red for the Sox. Some people think this gives her an edge, like the arty kids who cut class and smoke in the rundown courtyard attached to the science rooms. But it just makes her feel like someone, like herself.

When Kyle asks her out, it's monumental. They've been friends since Christmas, when they were assigned to the same geometry project. He began calling her every night during spring training and listened patiently as she listed all the reasons why she was in love with Trot Nixon and not the more typical Red Sox players who earn teenage-girl crushes, like Nomar Garciaparra or local boy Lou Merloni.

Later, she will learn that Kyle bought the tickets the week they went on sale, rising early on a Saturday and standing on Lansdowne Street for three hours, then carefully choosing an April series against Toronto. He is from Seattle and has only through Caroline been inducted into this strange obsessive world of the Boston Red Sox. The best seats he can afford from his after school job as a bag boy at Stop and Shop: front row, right field roof box.

The tickets sit on his desk for weeks, taunting him every time he

93

reaches for the phone. For 38 straight days, he chickens out. He gets to the point in their nightly conversations where he almost says it, the words on his lips, *will you go to a Sox game with me,* but he can't push them any further than that. He imagines them coming out all wrong — as if they are friends, as if he is taking the easy way out. It has to be a big gesture. It has to say "more than friends." On the other hand, in case he's read her wrong, he doesn't want to scare her off, demand a big commitment, whatever. He can't ever get the honey-like scent of her shampoo out of his nose, can't get her voice, complaining about the unfair domination of the New York Yankees, out of his ears.

They talk longer and longer, their phone calls stretching past ten, past twelve, past one, well into the early morning hours. They set records for longest conversations nightly, then break them the very next day. She tells him stories about her obsession with the 6-4-3 double play, the routine nature of the action moving it into the sublime. She talks about the beauty of a lefthander's arm crossing his body, the heady smells of wet grass and mustard and adrenaline. She talks and she talks until he falls in love, too, falls in love with her idea of baseball. He pores over the box scores, memorizes the statistics and the nicknames, follows the rest of this new town of his into a lifelong obsession with a team that's never quite reciprocated their passion.

When he is too tired to think straight, this is the moment he chooses to just do it. He begins casually, watching the early morning sun lighten the sky outside his bedroom window, over the rows of triple-deckers that stretch beyond the Dorchester house his parents bought a year ago before ever stepping foot on this side of the country.

She listens on the other end of the phone line, 4.7 miles away from him, cross-legged on the bench in the strange alcove on the third-and-a-half floor of the large house her grandparents snapped up for nothing at the height of the busing crisis, when no one wanted to send their kids to school in Boston. Now, not even a full generation later, she attends the best public school in the state, possibly the world. She can see Fenway Park from her third floor classrooms, stadium lights burning bright through the spring afternoon fog.

She listens to his voice through a haze of sleeplessness; she is still young enough to relish staying awake all night. She feels dangerous as she spins a strand of red-colored hair around her fingers and listens to the voice she created, the voice of a fellow Red Sox fan, obsessed with Pedro Martinez's ERA and Jose Offerman's on-base-percentage and the chances that the AL West will dominate the Wild Card race.

"Funny thing," Kyle says, and Caroline already feels her mouth moving into the right response for a laugh. "I have two tickets to Tuesday night's game against the Blue Jays. I thought that maybe we could go together." His voice is lower than she remembers, deeper than she expects. And then, quickly, he adds, "as friends."

"Awesome," she says. "I love the Sox. Of course I love the Sox. You've been hearing me say that for — how long?"

"Wait," he says, and she listens to the desperate silence that separates them, her stomach suddenly tight. "That's bullshit. I'm lying. Not about the tickets, but about the other thing. I don't want us to go as friends. I want this to be sort of like a date. No, not sort of. A date. An actual date. Because I think I'm in love with you, Caroline, and I'm trying to ask you out."

"Oh," she says, after a pause, her voice steady. "OK."

It's a big leap, a huge, massive jump over the yawning cavern between friend and boyfriend. But she's prepared for it. She's read *Sweet Valley High,* she watches "One Life to Live," she's heard similarly romantic stories of boys declaring their previously unrealized affections from almost every one of her friends. She's sixteen. And this is what happens when you're sixteen: boys suddenly declare they are in love with you.

Tuesday night is cold, threatening rain, and she tries to picture a clear sky, a sunny cool April night emerging from the fog as she directs her father through the twisty streets of Dorchester from a piece of paper covered in unfamiliar spidery boy handwriting. She only knows Kyle's numbers, the neat way he lines up his integers and equations on their math project, and nothing of the long thin scrawl that forms his words. When they find his house — tall, green, with a slate roof and small fenced-in yard — he's standing on the porch in a windbreaker and jeans and the same exact Red Sox cap as the one she wears. He looks similar, but different. Date Kyle.

"Daddy, this is Kyle." She stretches out his name, then jumps out of the car and pulls back her seat. He scrambles in behind her, then settles in the space between the two front seats, long legs squeezed in tight.

"Looks like it's going to be a good game tonight, if the rain holds off," her dad says, nodding in the rearview mirror. "You guys lucked out — Pedro is pitching." Kyle stutters some reply, calling her dad sir, and Caroline leans back with a smile at the formality of it all, at the nervous look that flashes across her father's face.

They get to Fenway in time for batting practice and edge their way into the clump of fans behind first base — little kids clutching scuffed baseballs, grown men with their thick stacks of cards — and then they lean their elbows on the padded green ledge that separates the fans from the field. Caroline stares out onto the field, at the players just beyond them, in their blue warm-up jackets and white baseball pants, like the ones her brothers wear for their high school team, but nicer, not polyester, made of a stronger material. She watches Valentin dash between second and third, Brian Daubach and Darren Lewis play catch on the edge of the infield grass, Varitek jog in from the bullpen, his pads and his catcher's mask tucked under his right arm.

"This is cool," Kyle says as he stares toward the Monster, and the change in his voice from confidence to awe triggers something within Caroline, reminds her of being eight years old, her ponytail threaded through the hole in the back of her Red Sox hat, her dad juggling a hot dog and a scorebook.

"That's right," she says. "This is your first time at Fenway."

She tries to see the Park through new eyes, the short blue-slatted seats crowded together, the dent in right field, the block letter abbreviations of American League cities running down the Green Monster. But she can't do it. It's way too familiar to her, this place she's been coming to, every spring, every summer, for as long as she can remember, this ballpark she's taken for granted, accepted as something that will always be here and accessible to her. There is talk, there is always talk, of tearing Fenway down, but Caroline chooses to ignore it and focus instead on how lucky she is to be in the same stands her great-grandfather once sat in and think that someday her grandchildren will come to games here, too.

After the Toronto players take batting practice, Kyle motions to their seats, and Caroline follows him upward, through the stadium, all the way to the roof box, where he buys them hot dogs and Cokes and a box of Crackerjacks, and she offers to pay, but he refuses, because that's what you do when you're sixteen and you're on a date. From up high, they can see everything, or they could see everything, theoretically, if a low fog hadn't settled over the edges of the ballpark and obscured even the Citgo sign from their line of sight. Instead, their point of view is confined solely to inside the ballpark, to what unfolds on the field below them, the Red Sox in their bright white uniforms emerging from the shadowy dugout and jogging out onto the pristine stretch of wet green grass. She shivers in her jacket, glad she wore jeans, a sweatshirt, warm socks on her first date. They are her favorite jeans, dark and straight, and they make her butt look good, and the sweatshirt has a zipper, with the words "Red" and "Sox" on either side, but still it seems wrong to wear clothes like this on a date, on her first date, even though her date is a ballgame. She wishes it were warmer, June, and during the day, maybe a nice sunny Saturday afternoon, where she could have worn shorts and a red tank top.

When four guys in matching vests begin singing the national anthem, Kyle rises to his feet, and Caroline bounces up beside him. Below, the players form two straight lines, and from up here, at this moment, all the Red Sox look the same, she can't see numbers or distinguishing details, can't tell Mike Stanley from Reggie Jefferson. It isn't until they break formation and jog out to their natural positions that she begins to pick them out. She's not keeping score tonight — too much to do with her hands, and Kyle is, right now, too much of a distraction for her to concentrate on every pitch — but her brain whirls through the batting lineup, figuring out the substitutions, happy to see her favorites — 'Tek behind the plate, Pedro on the mound, and of course, Trot Nixon in right field — are all starting. It makes the night, the date, perfect.

When it begins to rain in the top of the third, the stands below them empty out almost immediately, and the rest of the fans in their row quickly step over them and retreat backward, taking cover inside the confines of the concession tunnels. Kyle looks at Caroline, and she looks down at his hand closed tightly over hers, as it's been since Nomar batted in the bottom of the first, and they remain exactly where they are, in the seats he purchased for their grandeur as much as anything else, unwilling to sacrifice this hard-gained moment because of a little moisture. Their hats and their windbreakers protect them from the worst of it, and it's really not so bad. It reminds Kyle of Seattle, where it rained for the better half of ten years, and Caroline loves the beach more than any other place in the world except Fenway, and rain always feels like the light spray of the ocean, so she's good, too.

The rain falls, steady, and he puts his arm around her shoulder and she scoots closer to him, up against him, the metal armrest between them digging into her side. Below them, the umpires have begun to confer, and the Red Sox leave the field, their uniforms no longer spotlessly white, and the grounds crew is quick to replace them, yanking a tarp over the field.

Caroline sighs and thinks about the history quiz she needs to study for. Kyle reacts to her sigh, misinterpreting it, and pulls her even closer.

"Don't worry," he says, his hands rubbing her arms through all her layers of clothes. "This will end in a few minutes, they'll get the game in."

She smiles up at him, at the pattern the raindrops make against his face, the way they cling to his eyelashes and brighten his green eyes. She's never looked at a boy this closely before, and she's fascinated. The light shadow on his upper lip, the square shape of his jaw, the thickness of his eyebrows, how they almost come together in the middle of his face. She's enthralled by the small details, the differences that blur and then sharpen, and then suddenly he's kissing her. She forgets to close her eyes and is met with an extreme close-up of the pores of his cheeks before she clamps her eyes shut, his tongue moving around in her mouth, and he tastes of mustard (expected) and peanuts (expected) and something else not expected ... cough syrup? Listerine?

She's making out. The rain is falling on her and she's lost her hat, her hair is dark and loose and wet and streaked with red, and her jacket is soaked, her sweatshirt wet, she can feel the water through the legs of her jeans, chafing her skin. She's at Fenway Park, and she's being kissed by this boy who really, really likes her, maybe as much as she likes the Red Sox.

They are on TV. Everyone in the city of Boston watches them make out over the NESN broadcast during the rain delay, when there's nothing else to show but two teenagers, alone in the roof-box seats, furiously awkward in their unfamiliarity with each other, kissing desperately, his windbreaker emblazoned with their school name, the red streaks in her brown hair unmistakably her own, branding both of them totally, completely recognizable to everyone who knows either one.

It's not just TV. There's a picture of them in the *Boston Globe,* inside the sports page, that Caroline furiously rips out of her parents' paper, and then the neighbors', hiding both of them in the back of her closet.

"Caroline, phone!" Her father yells from downstairs. She pretends not to hear him, instead stands on the steps as she listens to the awkward turn his voice takes.

"Did you enjoy the game last night? Too bad it was rained out," her father is saying, and Caroline feels something in her stomach she can't identify, other than the fact that it's not good. She listens to the silence her father attempts to fill by clearing his throat, finally saying, "I guess she's getting ready for school. I'll tell her you called."

She waits at the top of the stairs for ten more seconds, then rushes down as quickly as she can. Her father stands at the bottom of the steps, and she knows from the look on his face that he was watching the game, and the bad feeling in her stomach triples.

"That was, uh, Kyle on the phone," he says. "I told him you'd see him at school."

"Thanks, Daddy."

She stands on the bottom step for a moment and considers faking a stomach ache, but decides she'd rather be out of this house as soon as possible, away from the photographs of her childhood, dance recitals, soccer games, birthday parties, reminders of the little girl she no longer is. She walks past the direct stop and down two blocks to where she can take the public bus, two buses, actually, so she won't run into anyone she knows, still keeping her head scrunched down over her history notes just in case.

"I didn't know you and Kyle were — together," her geometry teacher says to her in the hallway before homeroom, and the look on her face tells Caroline that she's proud to have taken some responsibility for this development, since she was the one who paired them up, made them spend so much time together on proofs and square roots.

It gets worse after that, and Caroline can't stop the redness from coloring her cheeks, bright as the streaks in her hair, seeping into her skin and staying there the whole rotten day. This is who she is. The girl caught making out with her boyfriend in Fenway Park, her Fenway Park, in front of everyone. And it feels awful. She remembers what it was like to not know who she was — could it only have been yesterday? — and suddenly she'd do anything to have that back. It has to be better than having who you are determined by something stupid you did at a Red Sox game with a boy you don't even know, not really, a boy who likes you much more than you're ready to be liked.

Kyle is ecstatic. All his worries, his fears about how to do this, how to move on to the next step, go from one date to dating, are instantly alleviated. Mass assumption being what it is, it's already an established fact. Caroline is his girlfriend. It may be by default, but it's still a fact, still something neither of them would have any luck denying. He coolly smiles when people talk about it in the hallways, when he's teased about it in gym class, at his locker. It's so public. You get a girl to kiss you at a Sox game, and suddenly, you're someone more than that quiet kid from Seattle.

He sees his future stretching ahead of him: they will have standing Saturday afternoon dates to catch a matinee at the cool Harvard Square theatre. He'll introduce her to Mongolian barbeque, and she'll make him eat clam chowder at that place in Copley Square she's always talking about. They'll double date with her best friend Sam and her boyfriend and his best friend Ryan and his girlfriend on alternating Friday nights.

All six of them will split a limo for prom, camp out at a table near the back and make fun of people who take the dance too seriously while wearing their fancy dresses and rented tuxes. During the summer, Caroline will spend a weekend with his family at the rented cottage in Harwich, and she'll share a room with his younger sister. They will go to as many Red Sox games as Kyle can afford, at least one a month, and watch plenty of others together on the couch in his family's den. He sees it all unfolding in front of him at the speed of light, high school as it's supposed to be.

Kyle is so caught up in his joy, he doesn't notice the look on Caroline's face when he catches her at her locker after the last bell rings, doesn't feel her hand flinch beneath his as he wraps his fingers around hers, then leans over to kiss her on her forehead, all cute, like he imagines a boyfriend would. Where he sees wide-open possibilities, she sees only closing spaces. She glances back at the picture hanging on her locker door, of Trot Nixon looking out at her, serious, his batting helmet on tight, his eyes focused on the goal ahead, the hit, the run, the win, and not for the first time, she is jealous. She longs to have something so concrete to work toward, a place like Fenway Park to do it within.

Caroline can't see the future, can't imagine what lies ahead of her, of them. She doesn't know that she won't feel so boxed in by this forever; she'll get used to Kyle, and as the months stretch on she'll even begin to like being his girlfriend, and as soon as she's comfortable with the idea, as soon as she starts to believe that maybe she loves, him, too, Kyle will break up with her. He'll claim it's just too hard to carry on something during the summer without the excuse of school to bring them together, but really, when he doesn't see her every day, Kyle will forget what it is about Caroline that made him think he was in love with her in the first place.

Standing in the hallway by her locker, she can't predict that he'll give her the tickets to the rescheduled game as a sort of consolation, but also because he doesn't like baseball without her all that much anyway, or that she'll go to the July game with her best friend Sam, and the two of them will sit at the edges of their seats, sweating in their red and blue tank tops under the hot summer sun. Fenway in the middle of summer is so different than Fenway in early spring: the smells, the sounds, the way the fans all crowd together, their expectations either swelling or deflating (this year swelling), adding an extra layer of energy to the air. The differences will have almost nothing to do with the lack of Kyle, or at least this is what Caroline will tell herself as Sam writes the players' names and numbers on the scorecard in her big bubbly handwriting as she sits in Kyle's seat.

"What are you thinking?" Kyle says, reaching out to pet her hair like a boy in a movie.

"Nothing," Caroline says.

Her red streaks burn into her skull under the weight of Kyle's hand, but she looks up at him and smiles, seeing the inevitability of her future, always to be decided by someone other than herself, captured within his green eyes.

Red Sox Poetry

JONATHAN P. WINICKOFF,
BOB FRANCIS,
AL BASILE,
AND RON SKRABACZ

Boston Spring

JONATHAN P. WINICKOFF

Sky shines Hancock blue
Near green lines gathered bunches
Budding Red Sox caps

It Ended in the
House that Ruth Built

BOB FRANCIS

The Sox
were caught in a box
because of a curse by a Babe
But, for a Schilling
the Yankees were willing
to throw a 7 game series away

Three Poems

AL BASILE

On Hearing Ned Martin's Comments During a Red Sox Game, July 26th, 1985

"They plan to strike on August sixth," he said,
"as if that date weren't bad enough already,
that's Hiroshima — or else good enough,
depending on the way you look at it."

Maybe it's tunnel vision that he had,
Ned Martin, thinking to compare a game
to that life-scorching day whose fire burns
us still, from here to Kingdom come. Maybe
as ritual of ash and cowhide dreamed
the people in the seats beyond the world,
he only meant to run down the statistics,
remind us of that old score, and the way
we settled it: how many left on base,
and when the pennant-clinching rally-killer came.
But probably he didn't think of that.
The date just stuck out in his memory
as a bad one — no sooner had the word
escaped his lips, when he remembered that
the home team won that war, and that you were
supposed to root for the home team every time,
and so he had to qualify the thought.
Now baseball's caught both East- and Western fancy,
and men who owe or lost their fathers' lives
to that forty-year-old midsummer's day
are playing on green grass between white lines
in Osaka and in Cincinnati.
There's no way for the ball to tell between them.
It had to be a blessing and a curse,

that August day, no matter how you look
at it. But it was Martin's instinct first
to tell us that the curse that fell on all
of us outweighs the blessing that fell to
the relatively few. For that, and for
remembering beyond the call of balls
and strikes in the high summer, thanks are due.
He has an instinct for the game, and more.

Red Sox Win, 2004

The only curse is thinking that you're cursed.
The losing of the battle in the mind:
the summoning of the image of the worst,
and, fearing it, yet loving it in kind.
The outcome tempts us from its side of time.
Says, "Worship me, and you can be as gods.
By naming it, you can insure the line
of what is yet to come. Forget the odds.
You can be certain. Just embrace your fate.
Be more than half in love with easeful death.
Give all your heart, and be its secret mate,
for it chose you before you drew a breath,
so special are you." These are simple lies.
You name only your loss. A future dies.

This Could Be the Year

The pitchers and the catchers
went south a week ago
and spring is going to come again
forget about the snow
the first pitch will be thrown out
the game will get in gear
this could be the year
All the true believers

have waited for so long
they've managed to stay faithful
as hopes have come and gone
they hang on to a vision
the dream is ever clear
this could be the year
Winners and losers
lovers and friends
there's a brand new beginning
if you stay past the end
There's better teams on paper
but that's not where it's played
and anything can happen
once a new start has been made
every record's even
and the moment's finally here
this could be the year
The odds might be against us
we've tried and failed before
we've come as close as you can come
and still been shown the door
when you've been just a strike away
there's nothing left to fear
this could be the year

The Bambino Curse That Disappeared

RON SKRABACZ

Listen, my children, and you shall hear
Of the Bambino Curse that disappeared.
Game Four of the Series, two thousand and four,
Hardly a fan forgets the score
And the Red Sox team of that special year.

They said to their fans, "If the Bosox march
To victory over the Cards tonight,
Hang a banner aloft in our Fenway Park
On the famed Green Monster as a signal bright!"

One in the first, and two in the third,
And none for the St. Louis hometown birds.
Ready to break from history's norm,
With every Boston fan waiting to swarm,
Letting all ride on Derek Lowe's arm.

And they said "Good start!" with Damon's long drive,
Silencing those on the St. Louis side,
Just as the moon rose over the river,
Where swinging bats met pitches delivered
From Jason Marquis, Cardinals fourth starter;
As fewer runs made each game harder;
Francona having to manage smarter;
So a 3–0 count meant no restriction,
And a two-run double for Trot Nixon.

Meanwhile, the outs continued to tally;
The Cards not hitting the horsehide sphere;
An entire nation beginning to cheer
This bunch of idiots at history's door,
About to walk from out of the valley;
An elusive quest of eighty-six years,
Not winning it since the First World War.

And they won their next flag after World War Two,   1946
With Ted and company back to play;
A wealth of hitters on display,
And twenty-game winners, Tex and Boo.
So they faced the Cards in that Series hunt,
And Game Three headlines blared "Ted Bunts!"
For six games they battled, tied three all,
With one game left to make the Curse fall,
But the eighth's now part of baseball lore
As Slaughter dashes from first to score —
Some still say that Pesky held the ball.

Ahead, though Impossible, lay the Dream;   1967
With a ninth-place mark the year before,
Sparked by a start from Billy Rohr;
This was the year, it was destiny's team.
Four teams, down to the wire they went,
As Boston completed its ascent,
The battle cry being, "Let's go Yaz!"
Watching him play with all that he has,
While winning our hearts, and the Triple Crown,
Along with the pennant for our Beantown;
And suddenly all our thoughts were spent
Just dreaming of something far away,
With thousands in churches to hope and pray;
A small request beseeched of Heaven —
But the Cardinals triumph in Game Seven.

Meanwhile, two rookies' careers take stride,   1975
With MVP stats, and new Red Sox pride
In Jim Rice and Fred Lynn, a pair revered,
Now playing outfield side by side.
And there were other reasons yet to cheer,
A pitching staff, like fine Chianti,
With veterans Wise and El Tiante.
Their Series foe, an impressive team,

The ever dangerous Big Red Machine.
The Sox, many said, would be swept in four,
But no one told Carbo, whose blast tied the score;
And lo! In Game Six, the Sox had new life;
A glimmer of hope to end their strife,
When Fisk hits the foul pole, while waving it fair.
But Morgan's bloop single cuts deep like a knife;
A seventh game loss, and still more despair.

    Then Boston takes two from the New York Mets,   1986
With Hurst, and then Clemens, the starting duo;
And with three games in Fenway, they'd two wins to go,
To halt seven decades of pain and regrets.
But the Mets won two, and like that it was tied,
'Til Bruce earned his second win in two tries;
And the Sox, a mere one game shy of the prize,
Looked to the Rocket to safeguard their quest.
They were one strike away when bad turned to worse,
For haunting them — shades of the fabled curse —
Is "the grounder," under a darkened sky,
And under the glove, then chasing in vain,
Allowing Game Seven; allowing more pain.
It's enough of a blow to make Boggs cry.

    T'was long ago that dreaded curse   2004
First cast its shadow onto Boston town.
No merriment or autumn mirth,
Just agony for eighty-six years,
Until this team blazed a new frontier,
A playoffs first in the second round.

    In Game One for the AL flag,   G1 ALCS
When they swaggered into New York town,
They saw their bats begin to sag
Against a perfect Moose for six;
And they found themselves trailing, eight to none,

Before they struck for seven runs,
A little too late to get some hits; And at evening's end they were
    one game down.

    In Game Two for the AL flag,   G2 ALCS
The hopes were high when Pedro took the mound,
But Lieber's gem was cause to brag,
For New York fans taunting "Who's your Daddy?"
And so, down two games to the Yankees

    They head back to their own home town.   G3 ALCS
And no one was safe in the Boston pen
As New York hammered the Fenway Wall,
To win Game Three by more than ten,
With twenty-two total hits in all.

    You know the rest. In the books you can read
How the Boston Red Sox were down by three,
How the Yankees had them set for a fall,
How behind from three no team could crawl,
'Til Ortiz went deep in the twelfth of Game Four.
In Game Five, with a bloop, he did it once more,
Paving the way for a Curt Schilling win,
Then winning it all, to the Yankees' chagrin.

    So through the streets they rode revered.
And on through the day frenzied fans partied down,
As every New England village and town
Shed tears of joy after eighty-six years.
A team for the ages, a team for Sox lore,
And a year that shall echo forever more!
For, borne on the heartbreak of the Past,
A euphoric high that's unsurpassed;
A new dawn of tales and bedtime stories
Of the Red Sox team that persevered,
Of suffering fans' first taste of glory,
And the Bambino Curse that disappeared.

Pitchers and Catchers Report

CECILIA TAN

The infield was baked red clay, that Georgia clay found on fields all over the country, brought places by the truckload. Kirby could smell it from the runway to the dugout, such an achingly familiar scent. It was the smell of Little League, and the field behind the school near his uncle's house, and learning to block balls in the dirt.

He emerged from the damp shade of the dugout into the bright but weak February morning sun. The breeze was cold but the grass green; a groundskeeper trimmed the verge beyond third base with a manual push mower. Beyond him, the jigsaw puzzle of advertising signs that made up the outfield wall shone bright and riotous. Kirby shifted his bag on his shoulder. He should have gone straight to his locker to put it down, but something made him want to see the field first.

The crunch of a set of spikes on concrete made him turn around, and there was Mike Greenwell, suited up in uniform pants and a ratty gray T-shirt. His dark moustache was matched not so much by a goatee as an untamed offseason lack of shaving.

"You're here a little early, aren't you?" Kirby said, without thinking.

"Eight a.m.? Not really," Greenwell replied as he went up the dugout steps to the grass.

"No, I mean, isn't it just pitchers and catchers today?"

"Like I have something better to do...?" Greenwell joked as he began a jog around the warning track.

It was only later, when Kirby found the locker with his name on it and saw Greenwell's was across from his, that he realized he hadn't introduced himself. *Wouldn't want to seem like a brown-noser,* he thought, after the fact. The locker, the one with "Wilcox" over it, written with a magic marker on a wide strip of what looked like medical tape, had a pile of brand new catching equipment in it. The elation over the new equipment almost overcame the letdown of seeing that his locker tag was temporary. Of course it was. This was his first invite to Red Sox spring training.

Catchers tended to get the invite to the big club sooner than other position players. It was just math — there were so many pitchers who needed to work out, put in bullpen sessions, non-roster invitees auditioning for jobs. Probably more that thirty pitchers in camp right now. Maybe forty. Prospects were there, too, starters and bullpen guys — just pitchers everywhere. That meant a lot of catching to be done. Kirby knew that, but he'd still felt privileged to get the word that, just a year out of rookie ball, he would be lockering with the likes of Mike Greenwell.

Other guys were filtering in now, some he knew from rookie ball, some not. Now introductions were okay, he decided, since they were mostly new guys, both the pitchers and the catchers. Ever since Tony Peña left, there had been something of a revolving door at catcher for the Sox, and every guy there was aware of it. Kirby's heart started to beat harder just thinking about it. Who knew? Make an impression on someone, maybe someone else tweaks a muscle, anyone could be behind the plate on Opening Day, wasn't that right? He pictured himself crouching behind the dish, Roger Clemens on the mound, the big green wall visible through the bars of his mask, Clemens' leg kick. . . .

There was Clemens now, big Texas guy, his hair in need of a trim, shaking hands and exchanging back slaps with some of the other players near his locker. *Yes,* thought Kirby, *this is where I belong.* He decided to dump the worry about brown-nosing and went to join the circle around Roger's locker, but halfway there he saw a satin-jacketed coach tacking up a white piece of paper. There were always too many coaches and assistant coaches to keep track of in Spring Training, but anyone with gray hair and a field jacket was probably in the know. Kirby veered toward the bulletin board. The notice had the day's workout schedule and rotation. He and Clemens were in a group together. His chest swelled with pride. *Maybe they do like me, after all,* he thought.

An hour later he was in the bullpen, his gear on, while Clemens and two other starters prepared to take the mound under the watchful eye of a coach. Kirby kept forgetting the names of the other two guys. One of them he should have known, too, because they had faced each other in college. But try as he might, the name Gar Finnvold was too ridiculous to stick in his brain. The other one, same problem: Nate Minchey, for whatever reason it was like these two guys could not be for real. Finnvold took the mound first and tweaked something in his landing leg within the first five pitches. He and the coach went off in search of the trainer, and Minchey took a seat on the bench to wait for his return.

"C'mon," Clemens said to Kirby, "I'll have a go. It's not like I'm really going to air it out on the first day."

Kirby crouched behind the plate and tamped down the spike of anxiety that rose up in his throat. He told himself he had caught plenty of fireballers in his time and besides, as Clemens had said, he wasn't going to be trying to light up the radar gun today.

Still, the first fastball popped loudly in Kirby's mitt, and he felt the sting in his left hand. He plucked the ball out and lobbed it back to Clemens who stood waiting at the bottom of the mound, his glove bobbing impatiently for the return throw.

The next pitch was the same, and soon he and Kirby sank into a rhythm. All Kirby did was think about catching it, throwing it back, catching it, throwing it back. That was plenty to think about. He didn't know Clemens' form, his habits, his tendencies, any of that stuff. His job right now was singular: get the ball back to Roger.

"All right if I try Mister Splittee?" Roger called as the ball sailed back to him.

"You sure?" Kirby asked, tipping his mask onto the top of his head so he could talk. Pitchers typically didn't start on the breaking stuff until later in the spring. But maybe Roger didn't count the split-finger fastball as a breaking pitch.

"No, are *you* sure?" was Roger's reply, "Meat?"

"Bring it on," Kirby said with a smile as he yanked the mask back down. He pounded the glove for emphasis.

The first one, as Fate would have it, got by him. Bounced in the dirt right at the plate, and then went through his legs and hit the chain link fence, startling some reporters on the other side. Kirby felt his cheeks burn under his mask. *That's baseball,* he repeated to himself, the mantra he had learned long ago when he discovered it could be a humiliating game. *That's baseball.*

No more balls got by and after a few more minutes of that, Roger was done. Minchey shrugged, not wanting to throw until the coach came back. So Roger and Kirby sat together on the bench, companionably sweaty and drinking water out of Gatorade cups.

"So how did it look to you?" Roger asked.

"Good," Kirby replied.

"Good?"

"Good." Kirby shrugged. "I got no basis of comparison."

Roger crumpled the lime green cup in his hand and tossed it on the ground. "You were a Gator, weren't you."

"How did you know that?" Kirby had, in fact, gone to the University of Florida, Gainesville.

"I play golf with a sports administrator from there, nobody you'd know," he said, which didn't answer the question. "Did you always catch or were you converted?"

Was I that bad? Kirby wondered. "I caught and pitched in high school...."

"Red, hey Red!" Roger shouted to a coach passing by and gave him an exaggerated hieroglyphics-style shrug. "What gives?"

The coach, a wizened fellow with a shock of white hair Kirby didn't recognize, pointed back the way he had come.

"C'mon," Roger said then, giving Kirby a slap on the shoulder, and jogged off to the practice field where the next phase of the workout was beginning.

That night Kirby found himself at the local steakhouse the players favored, sitting around the square of a bar in the center with six or seven other guys, all pitchers except for him. He ordered a beer, a steak, and a tall glass of iced tea, "hold the tea." The bartender was a cute blond who didn't get it, but the pitcher on his left, a bullpen hopeful named Hiram Green, burst out laughing.

"Just do it, honey," Green said to her. "In fact, put it on my tab."

That got a smile out of Kirby. Green, despite his name, wasn't — he had been bouncing around the league for a good number of years already before getting the invite to Red Sox camp. Kirby didn't know much about him.

When the ice came, Kirby clamped his swollen left hand around the glass, and sighed.

"You catching Roger today?" Green asked.

"Yeah."

"Thought it was you. Can't really tell you guys apart with the fucking masks on, of course. What number you wearing?"

"Eighty seven."

"They gave me sixty seven." Hiram shuddered. "If I make the team I hope I get to switch it up."

"Why?"

"How old are you? Aw, you would have been only two. But sixty seven, that was a cursed year for the Red Sox, didn't you know?"

"Oh yeah?" One of the younger guys down the bar said. "I'm wearing eighty six! Gah!"

Kirby sipped his beer in silence while the pitchers indulged their superstitions. As a catcher, he was used to this kind of thing. Pitchers, when in groups, invariably talked about three things besides women: breaking balls, jinxes, and hitting. Yes, hitting. Even American League pitchers seemed obsessed with it. The rumor that Major League Baseball was going to institute interleague play during the regular season within a few years persisted, and of course here in Spring Training, when they played a National League team, they would use National League rules.

So Kirby wasn't surprised when, halfway through his steak, the pitchers started talking about wanting more cage time. "Yeah, I want to get my cuts." Hiram said. "But I'm a bullpen guy. Like I'm going to be out there more than one inning anyway."

"Don't say that, Green," a blond, red-faced lefthander named Jones, said, a little breathless. "Some of those split squad games, they don't bring that many guys. If you come in to face the last batter of an inning, and then have to pitch the next inning, and the pitcher's spot comes up to bat...."

"Keep dreamin'," Hiram replied. "'Cause that's the only way you or I are getting any licks in this spring. Really. No way, José."

One of the Latin pitchers jumped in at that, though Kirby hadn't determined if the guy's name was José or not. He stopped listening. Everyone knew pitchers couldn't hit. The National League clung to their stupid rule out of tradition, but they were pretty much the only ones at this point. Kirby had been a fairly good pitcher in his time, but one of the reasons he had given it up was that his hitting talent would have gone to waste. Well, that was the rational reason they gave. The less rational reason was that he somehow knew, because he could hit, that he did not belong in the fraternity of pitchers. His eyes scanned the bar. Where were all the other catchers tonight? Did they have some other watering hole he didn't know about?

The pitchers around him, egged on by booze and the presence of the blond bartender — her baby blue shirt seeming to grow tighter as the evening wore on — were now actually bragging to one another about which one was a better hitter than the next. Kirby put a twenty dollar bill on the bar and stood up to leave.

"You ain't goin' now, are you, man?" said José, or whatever his name was.

"Catchers have early *cage time* tomorrow," he said, unable to resist making it a subtle dig.

"Okay, mister high and mighty," said Hiram. "But just wait until you see how I hit."

Kirby didn't mask his chuckle, which was maybe a tad on the condescending side. He figured it was all in good fun, but he hadn't counted on how much Hiram had drunk, or why Hiram — despite deceptive stuff and a high strikeout to inning ratio — never stuck with a club.

"What are you laughing at? Are you laughing at me?" Before Kirby could answer, Hiram proclaimed, "I'm sure I hit better than you pitch, meat."

"Don't bet on it," Kirby said and walked out.

The next day went much like the first: bullpen sessions, fielding practice, wind sprints, the usual. It was some time around noon when Kirby realized he was the subject of a larger than usual amount of looks.

"What is that all about?" he asked Roger, as they walked back to the foul line to start the next wind sprint.

"Heard any trade rumors?"

"No."

"Have a hot date last night?"

"No."

"Then it's probably nothin'."

But when Kirby got back to the clubhouse, he found Hiram and a small cabal of pitchers hanging around his locker. A twenty dollar bill was tacked next to Kirby's name tag.

"So, when are we getting it on, amigo?" Hiram said, his smile and arms wide. He was wearing only a towel around his waist and his shower flip flops.

"Sorry, Hiram, you're not my type," Kirby replied, drawing guffaws out of some of the guys.

"No, no, man, our bet."

"What bet?"

"Don't you remember? At the bar last night, you bet me twenty dollars that you can pitch better than I can hit." Hiram indicated the sawbuck with one long finger.

"No, I didn't," Kirby said. "That twenty was to pay my bill."

"Don't you remember? I said I was paying for you last night."

Kirby paused for a moment. That wasn't the way he remembered it. But his argument clearly wasn't going to get him anywhere, not if they were all in on it. He just wasn't sure what kind of clubhouse prank this was leading to. It wasn't that he didn't expect a little hazing — that came with the territory — but he really didn't know where this was going. "That was just talk," Kirby said, pushing his way through the group to the locker. He sat down on the stool and started unlacing his spikes. They were caked with red infield dirt.

The group did not disperse, looking to Hiram to take the lead. "All I know is, we have a bet, you and me, and we ought to find a time and place to see who wins it." There were murmurs of approval from the others. "I mean, who said pitchers couldn't hit?"

Did I say that? Kirby wondered. He didn't think he'd actually said it. "Later, Hiram. I gotta go lift."

"Oh, right, build up those muscles so you can get that fastball of yours by me," the pitcher sniggered, then sauntered away.

By the time the regular position players showed up at camp, Kirby's hands, knees, and throwing arm were more sore than they had ever been in his life. Thank goodness for the trainers, who had a ready supply of ice, liniment, analgesics, and rub downs. He didn't mind being sore when it meant being taken care of so well. And he was catching Roger Clemens every other day, which he could tell his grandchildren about. All in all, Kirby was in baseball-player heaven, well, except for one thing: Green and his bet.

Somehow things had escalated to the point where now half the pitchers in camp were getting ready to take swings against him, and the other half were placing bets.

He knew it was at the point of no return when during one of those wind sprint walk-backs, Clemens himself said, "Heck, I'd like to get in there and take some cuts against you myself."

"Can you hit?" Kirby replied.

"I dunno," Clemens shrugged. "I've been in the American League all my life. But I never back down from a challenge."

Kirby sighed. There hadn't been any challenge, but everyone was acting like there was, and in a team situation you had to go with the group's idea of reality. "Can I ask you something?"

"Sure." The Rocket spat onto the grass.

"Can you show me how you throw the splitter?"

A couple of days later in the showers, Kirby snapped Hiram on the ass with a towel and said, "So, when are we getting it on?"

"Whenever you're ready," Hiram replied, clapping his hands with glee, ignoring the welt on his ass, and scrubbing his head with vigor under the spray of the high showerhead.

"What about tomorrow, since it's a light day." Kirby started the flow on the next showerhead. They were the big ones, like sunflowers, and they never ran out of hot water.

"Sorry, couldn't hear you," Hiram said, shaking water from his hair and ears like a dog. He raised his voice. "Did you say *tomorrow*?"

"Yeah." Kirby grabbed the soap and began to lather his chest, gently because there were a couple of bruises there from getting crossed up and taking bouncers in the dirt off his equipment. "I hear there's some other guys want a piece of me, too."

"Yeah, me!" shouted José — it turned out his name was José — from across the cinderblock room.

"Fine." Kirby ducked his head under to wet his hair and then turned to Hiram. "Get as many guys together as you want."

Hiram had raised an eyebrow and was unsure what to say now that Kirby had made such a dramatic about face. "So what's the bet then? You gonna pay us each twenty bucks if we get a hit off you?"

Kirby shook his head. "Even a blind chipmunk finds a nut sometimes."

"So, what, no lucky hits?"

"Hiram, Hiram," Kirby said, not sure where the confidence in his voice was coming from, since he didn't actually feel it. "Have you really thought about how this is going to work? We gotta do it schoolyard style."

"What do you mean?"

"Any ground ball on the infield is an out, any pop up is an out. Line drives, anything that lands on the warning track, hits the wall, or goes over, is a hit. You guys get twenty seven outs. Every three outs clears the bases." He ducked his head again then came out blinking water out of his eyes. "I'll give you twenty bucks for every run you score."

"You're on," Hiram said, and they shook on it, ghetto style, to the whooping of José in the background.

Kirby found, much to his annoyance, that he could not sleep that night. He was housed in a two-star motel a couple of miles from the park, the same place most of the other low-paid players and coaches stayed. Nice little place, the kind with a breakfast room and a coffee dispenser that ran 24 hours. Kirby was as perky as the coffee when midnight came around. It wasn't as if he really cared whether Hiram, or any of the other pitchers, got a hit or a run off him. It was Hiram's ego, not Kirby's, that had a lot at stake.

But something one of the coaches had said in the lobby had gotten him worrying. As he was grabbing a little iced tea from the dispenser there, Red had come up and wished him good luck.

"Oh, you know about it?" Kirby had said.

"Kiddo, everyone knows about it. Didja think you were just going to waltz out there and no one was gonna care?"

"Well, I...."

"Even the groundskeepers are going to be out there. Heh, should be fun."

Kirby lay in bed after that, wondering how he could have missed the fact that he was now the center of everyone's attention. That hadn't been his intent. He just wanted to get it over with, in fact, so that he would stop being the recipient of so much attention. But he couldn't call it off now; he had to get out there and do it. Just like any other day in base-ball, he told himself. Sure, it was something out of the routine, but it was still baseball. The whole key to success was just being in the moment and doing your best. Right?

The next morning he arrived at his locker to find the other catchers — or someone — had festooned it with red, white, and blue bunting, and there was a ball stuffed into one of his cleats. He shook his head — he knew what the ball meant. In the old days, before strict pitching rota-tions, managers used to leave a ball in the shoe of that day's starting pitcher so he'd know it was him.

There was a glove there, too, a pitcher's glove. Kirby picked it up gingerly, as if it might be booby-trapped, but it appeared to be free of joy buzzers, roaches, or dog poop. He turned the glove over and saw the name "Clemens." He had a moment of panic, wondering who stole it from Roger's locker and looking around to see if he might be able to slip the glove back in there without anyone noticing. But then Clemens himself came up beside him, clapped Kirby on the shoulder, and said, "I thought you might need that."

"Holy crap, Rocket, thanks."

"No problem, man. Now let's get out there."

Kirby found it hard to concentrate on the workouts that day. He had to catch Hiram, for one thing, and everywhere he went, people were full of cracks and comments. He found himself blushing under his mask a lot. He tried to shut it out, stay within himself, but he couldn't.

He paid for it when catching Roger in the bullpen around noon. They got out of synch, Kirby got crossed up, and Roger let go a forkball when Kirby was expecting the fastball, or maybe it was the other way around. Either way, Kirby didn't see what he expected, caught the pitch awkwardly, and the next thing he knew Roger was leaning over him asking "Are you okay?"

"I'm fine, I'm fine," he said automatically. It's what he and every other athlete always says when asked "are you okay" despite the fact that he was probably not "okay." Then the trainer and some coaches were there with more specific questions like "Can you stand up" and "Can you take your glove off" — the answer to both being "not yet." Kirby was hunched over the hand inside his glove, his eyes squeezed shut like he could somehow wish away the pain if he just tried hard enough.

Now there was the long walk from the bullpen, along the foul line, down the dugout steps, and Kirby felt like if every eye hadn't been on him before, they were all watching him now. The trainer walked on one side and Roger on the other, holding him by the elbows like it was his leg he had hurt, not his fingers. The midday sun shone like a spotlight, and it seemed to Kirby as if the whole camp had paused to watch his slow march to the trainer's room. The normal sounds of a spring workout, the smack of games of catch, the steady chop of wood in the batting cage — all were silent.

As they went up the tunnel, he thought he heard Hiram's voice from across the grass, "Aw, *man!*"

Twenty minutes later Kirby was breathing a sigh of relief. They had an X-ray machine right there, and nothing was broken. Hell, it was only a sprained pinky. He might have dislocated it, but the pinky had popped right back in. He had it wrapped in ice and resting on a shelf as high as his shoulder when Roger came in.

"So, Doc, what's the prognosis?"

"He won't be catching for a while," the trainer said.

"Yeah, but can he still pitch?"

The trainer looked at Roger like he had grown another head.

"Can you just tape the two fingers together?" Kirby asked. "I don't really use my pinky very much."

"You're a catcher, right?"

"Right." Kirby caught Roger gesturing at him from behind the trainer's back. "Am I cleared to do other things besides catch, though? Like can I still do my running and lifting?"

"Oh, I suppose," the trainer said with a sigh and reached for a roll of white medical tape. "Let me see it."

And so it was that Kirby "Nine Fingers" Wilcox, pumped full of ibuprofen and wearing Roger Clemens' glove, took the mound in Fort Myers to face a motley lineup of eleven pitchers who were all milling around the on deck circle, fiddling with their stiff, new batting gloves and their borrowed bats. Three different catchers sat in the shade of the visitor's dugout with their shin guards on, playing rock, paper, scissors to determine who caught first.

Kirby hadn't expected to have a catcher. Then, to his surprise he saw he had fielders, too. Scott Hatteberg, another catcher, stood at first base, one of the other guys out of the minors at third. And how about

Mike Greenwell and Roger standing in left center, talking? When they saw him look back at them from the mound, they jogged apart. Kirby blinked. Roger was going to play center field?

There were whistles and cat calls from the rest of the team, players, coaches, and other employees sitting behind home plate, but back about twenty rows so they were in the shade of the roof. Rich Rowland crouched behind the plate and gave Kirby the sign to start his warm-up pitches. Red stood close by, working his chaw absentmindedly, until Kirby had thrown his eighth warm-up pitch, when Rowland and Red shouted simultaneously, "Coming down." And just like before a real inning, the catcher threw the ball to second base, and then Red stepped up in the role of umpire.

Hiram walked to the plate, unperturbed by this turn of events. Kirby took a deep breath and tried to put out of his mind the thought that everyone else knew more about what was going on than he did. He cleared his brain of all thoughts except being grateful to have a catcher. Having a target made it so much easier.

He kicked and threw his fastball. Hiram stared at the ball, it hit the glove, and Red called out "Hype!" and raised his fist.

Hiram waggled the bat, exchanging looks with his teammates, the other pitchers who had now taken seats in the home dugout. "You've seen him now, you've seen him now," one of them shouted.

Kirby kicked and dealt. This time Hiram swung late and missed.

"Hype-*oo!*" Red shouted.

"What was that!" Hiram called to Kirby, jokingly, as if Kirby had thrown some trick junk pitch. But it was just a fastball, a plain fastball.

Kirby blinked; Rowland had just put down a sign. Two fingers. And then Kirby heard Roger's voice from behind him in center, where he had probably seen the sign, too, shouting, "Come on, give it to him, now, come on now!"

Kirby threw the forkball. He held onto it a tad too long, and the ball bounced in the dirt, but Hiram had started his swing early, and he golfed at it and missed.

"Hy-ee! Yer out!" Red screamed and gave a theatrical flourish as he pumped his fist.

Hiram didn't joke now. He stared at Kirby all the way back to the dugout. The guys on the bench gave him a hard time, some of them imitating that last duck-assed swing. José was next.

Rowland called for the fastball and Kirby threw it. And again, and again. And José went down swinging, though it was a better swing. Hoots were coming from the stands now — "I told you none of you could hit the side of a barn!" — and the pitchers were starting to sit up a bit on the bench. Their jocularity was undiminished, but each man began to pay a bit more attention to Kirby's delivery. They groaned wildly when the third of their number also went down on strikes.

Rowland jogged out to the mound. "So do we take a break between innings or what?"

"I just need some water," Kirby said, and Rowland motioned for one of the bat boys to bring him a bottle. He took a swig, resettled his cap, and was ready to throw again.

The first batter to hit a ball fair came in the fourth inning, when Hiram came to bat again. This time he swung late at a pitch, but got wood on the ball, and hit a soft three-hopper right to Hatteberg at first.

"Thank god!" Roger shouted. "We're starting to get bored out here!" But he didn't sound bored.

Kirby, for his part, had stopped counting the outs. There had been no one on base so there had been no need to know when the third out came and cleared them. The breaks were brief. In one, a new catcher came in and had a brief chat with Rowland, but to Kirby nothing had changed. He would set, look for the glove, throw, and then wait for the ball to come arcing back to him. Sometimes he would grip the ball across the seams, sometimes along the seams — that was the only change in his world. Oh, and sometimes the batters were lefthanded, but even that didn't seem to matter since none of them could hit him.

When it got to be the end of the sixth, he started to hear the shouting again. There was a lot more now, and much more of it was aimed at him. "C'mon Kirby, attaboy!" Things like that, from voices he did not recognize. But it echoed against the inside of his skull — he heard without noticing. He was too intent on just keeping his motion the same, his leg kick, his follow through.

Here was Hiram again. There were no jokes from him this time, no smile on his face. He dug in and waggled the bat. Kirby blinked as his brain did the math. If they had eleven men in their lineup, and this was the start of the third time through, then Hiram was the twenty third man.

Perhaps the thought broke his rhythm or perhaps he was tiring, but the next two pitches were wide of the strike zone by an obvious margin.

"Whatsa matter, Wilky?" Hiram called, suddenly animated again. "Afraid I've figured you out?"

The catcher called for time and came jogging up to Kirby. Kirby was shocked to realize it was Hatteberg, which meant someone else was at first base now. He filed that away in his brain as he tried to hear what Hatty was saying. "I'm flying open?"

"Yeah, your shoulder. Down and hard. Come on." He gave Kirby a pat on the butt and then jogged back behind the plate. Kirby blinked. It was word for word what he had told many pitchers, many times. How surreal.

Hatty pointed at him with the glove, pounded his fist in it, and called for the fastball.

Kirby kicked, fired, it went in for a strike, right down Broadway. Hiram shook his head as if to clear it. Kirby could almost imagine what Hatty was saying, under his breath, because it was what Kirby would say. "You just don't expect it to be right there, do you?"

So now, come back with it again, or try the splitter? The splitter. Kirby nodded, kicked, and brought his arm through his motion. Hatty caught the ball just below Hiram's knees and then whipped his glove up an inch or two.

"H — " Red began, but then thought better of it. "Ball three."

"Nice frame job," Hiram said to Hatteberg.

Kirby kept his eyes trained on Hatteberg's hand and his glove. *Okay, again.* This time Hiram tried his golf swing again, but fouled the ball off. Full count.

Come back with the fastball, Kirby thought, and nodded as Hatteberg thought the same thing. Kirby was already visualizing Hiram's swing, how he would swing late on this extra-fast fastball, and have to go back to the bench, defeated. The sun was hot — the morning breeze always died by mid-afternoon — and Kirby could feel sweat making the sleeves of his undershirt stick to his armpits. *Here it comes,* he thought.

As soon as he released the ball, he knew he had made the classic mistake. Trying to put a little extra on it, he had muscled up and instead slowed the ball down, flattened it out. Hiram put a huge swing on it and the ball sailed up and up, straight over Kirby's head.

"Roger!" Kirby wasn't the only one shouting.

Clemens turned this way and that, everyone in the whole ballpark thinking that's the toughest play a center fielder has to make, the ball hit straight to the middle, but Roger kept retreating and finally turned, backpedaling and then stretching out over his head, giving half a leap and snaring the ball in the edge of the webbing of his glove. He somersaulted backwards and then sat up, holding the glove up in the air while everyone whooped and hollered.

"Hot shit! Sign that kid up!"

"Rocket, who knew?"

"Yahoo!"

And Hiram's voice, too. "No way! No fucking way!" He had already been past second base when Roger made the catch, and he jogged past the mound on his way back to the dugout, but did not make eye contact with Kirby.

Kirby waited for the ball to come back to him, then got a drink. He glanced into the pitchers' dugout and found most of them sitting in dejected postures, batting gloves strewn about. Hiram was shaking his head and still saying, "No way, no way."

Red hollered. "Four outs to go."

José stood in, and barely waved at three pitches before going sheepishly back to the bench.

"Aw, c'mon!" Hiram chastised him. "Didn't you see that drive! We're getting to him now!" But none of the others looked like they really wanted to go through with it. "Gimme that bat."

Kirby just shrugged when Red gave him a look like "is this in the rules?" If Hiram wanted to make the last three outs, that was fine with Kirby. Hiram was jazzed now, surely he'd overswing — and indeed, they got him to pop up a high fastball which Hatty caught right between the plate and the backstop.

"Two to go," Red said.

"Dammit," Hiram said, digging in again.

They went after him again, with a similar result, only this time the pop up went to Kirby himself. He felt it land in his glove and his pinky twinged horribly. He shook it off, climbed back up on the mound, and waited for Hiram to get back in the box.

This time he tried to start him off with a splitter, but it bounced in the dirt, Hiram didn't swing, and it was ball one. Kirby tried to come back with the fastball but it sailed outside, and it was ball two.

Hatteberg visited the mound, his red eyebrows pale in the strong sunlight. "Do you want to walk him?"

"What?"

"Is this the unintentional intentional walk, or are you really just so gassed that you can't hit the strike zone anymore?"

"I don't know. How many pitches do you think I've thrown?"

"Ninety? A hundred?"

They both thought about that a moment and Hiram shouted, "Come on, guys, we haven't got all day!"

"Jerk," Hatteberg said, but where only Kirby could see it. "Hang in there, let's get him."

But the next one was a fastball that Kirby overthrew and Hatteberg had to jump up out of his crouch to make sure it didn't hit Red.

Hiram began to crow. "He's got a perfect game on the line and he's going to walk me? Lil' ol' me?"

Kirby coughed. *Perfect game, my ass,* he thought. *This isn't a game. In fact, I don't know what it is.* Then he realized he was about to walk a pitcher, for gods sake, and if there are cardinal sins in baseball, that had to be one of them, no matter what the situation.

What am I doing out here, anyway? he thought. *This is all about Hiram's ego, not mine. Maybe I ought to just cookie one in there, let him hit the damn thing, that'd make a good story, wouldn't it? How I no-hit them all day until the very last out ...?* It was tempting, like he could be Fate for one moment.

But then he could hear Roger screaming. "Come on, damn it, Kirby, let's finish this and go home! Just put him away already! Don't make me come over there and do it!"

And the people in the stands, the other players, the office girls, everyone, they were all shouting. It didn't matter this was just a lark, that this didn't "count." Kirby suddenly didn't want to disappoint anyone, either.

Just throw the ball, he thought. *That's the only part I can control. Just throw the ball.*

Hatty dropped down two fingers. Kirby adjusted his grip, kicked his leg, and let it fly.

Hiram, who had gotten stiff standing there while Kirby mused, swung late, just got a little wood on it, and it was another pop up. Hatteberg screamed "I got it! I got it!" He flung the mask away so hard it hit Red in the stomach and doubled him over, and then Hatteberg did get it, the ball landing nicely in the round pocket of his mitt.

Hatteberg leaped in the air — "Yes!" — and ran to give Kirby the ball. Kirby had pumped his fist as the ball came down, but now seemed bewildered by the rushing, jumping teammates all around, pounding him on the back and shouting. The next few minutes were a blur of Hiram shaking his hand and saying well, you know, pitchers can't hit worth a lick, and Roger signing the ball and getting the other guys to add their signatures to it, and asking what the date was so it could be written on there, and more slaps on the back and invitations for dinner, drinks, rounds of golf on the next off day, as the whole gaggle of players finally made their way back into the clubhouse to get out of the afternoon heat and humidity.

So it was, flushed with success but with his pinky and his arm hurting like never before that Kirby Wilcox came to his locker to stow the souvenir ball, only to find all his gear neatly packed, the bunting gone, his name gone — though the twenty was still there. Hatteberg stared with his mouth open, but Roger just shook Kirby's hand — the one without the sprained finger. "Thanks. That was fun. Keep the glove."

It was Red who came by and told him he was on the disabled list, officially, and so was being transferred to minor league camp. Kirby gave the twenty to the bat boy on his way out the door, as he repeated to himself over and over, *That's baseball, that's baseball.*

Inheritance

LENORE MYKA

I saw Yvette waiting for me as the cab pulled through the gates of Sherwood Manor, the assisted living facility where she lived. She was perched on one of the marble benches located just outside the front entrance, her hands folded carefully in her lap, ankles crossed, feet just dangling above the ground, face tilted toward the autumn sun, posture perfect. A picture of serenity to the untrained eye, but her stillness didn't fool me. I knew she'd been waiting there long before our scheduled hour and was now irritated because I was running late.

As the car pulled nearer, I saw her fingers flicker, a scissoring motion at the air. It was the only sign I needed to know I was in the doghouse.

I greeted her as I stepped out of the cab. "Hello, Yvette!" I said in the chirpiest tone I could muster. "Sorry to make you wait. I had a meeting with the vice president that went over- "

"— I have an hour," she said, standing. She glanced at the delicate gold watch that fit loosely around her wrist. "Actually, I take that back. I have forty-seven minutes before game-time."

"There's a game tonight?" I asked, but she had already pattered off, her steps short and fast.

Yvette was through the entrance of Sherwood Manor before I had finished paying the cabby. The elevator doors opened just as I caught up to her.

It may not have seemed like it on this particular afternoon, but Yvette was by far my favorite assignment for work. Graduate of the Class of '43, she was one of the alumna I was supposed to visit occasionally and hit up for a big donation to the women's college where I worked. The reality of my visits, however, was that I never actually asked her

129

for money and she never actually wrote a check, at least not in front of me. My boss had yet to question why I logged so much time on a person from who I hadn't gotten a cent. But visiting Yvette was one of the few pleasures I reaped from my work and so I figured I'd keep going until told otherwise.

Unlike the other alumnae I visited who tried to engage me in lively discussions about politics, gardening, travel, American history, and the latest alumni events at the college, Yvette talked only of two things: her life and the Red Sox. Sometimes, it was hard for me to distinguish between the two, so often did the lines between Yvette's personal history and the history of her beloved baseball team blur. There was the time in 1954 when she convinced someone on the management team to let her throw the first pitch of the opening game at Fenway and hit the umpire (who'd been standing ten yards to the left of home plate) in the head; the time in 1962 when her father was within hours of purchasing the team only to have the deal scrapped at the last minute; the time she took her seven- year-old nephew to his very first game in seats behind home plate and watched to her dismay as he got sick on popcorn, soda, and hotdogs, forcing them to leave before the top of the fifth. I'd heard them all.

Most of my visits to Yvette followed a distinct routine: after the usual greetings and formalities, I'd be seated and served a glass of sherry. Yvette would then launch into a series of stories, I would listen and laugh, and eventually she would grow distracted and tired of talking, at which point she'd kick me out, usually five minutes before game time.

"You know, I appreciate punctuality in a person," Yvette said now, her eyes fixed on the numbers as they lit up above the door. She was barely five feet tall but her presence was enormous; it suffocated me in that small space. I knew that apologies were wasted on her, so instead I bit my lip. But Yvette surprised me that afternoon and did something she'd never done before: she let me off the hook.

"No bother," she said conspiratorially, patting my arm. "I prefer you over all of the others. Especially that one with teeth like a mule."

"Barbara."

Yvette chuckled, shaking a finger at me. "So you know! Yes. That's the one. *Bar-ba-ra.*"

My boss.

"She drives me batty, that one."

"You're not the only one she drives batty," I blurted, unable to contain myself.

For me, Barbara represented all that was bad about my job. She was a woman who began each and every day by eagerly reading the obituaries listing in the newspaper. Her goal: to see if any of our alumnae had kicked the bucket. "There's a silver lining to every tragedy," she liked to say by way of rationalizing her vulture fundraising techniques, and had let it be known on more than one occasion that she was disappointed in my lack of similar enthusiasms. "You're not going to get director positions with an attitude like that," she'd warn me. Little did she know that my morning ritual began with scanning the "Help Wanted" section of the *Boston Globe*.

"I hate when she comes calling," Yvette said. She fluttered her eyelashes, pursing her lips like a suction cup. Flawless Barbara. "'Oh, dear Ms. Bouchard, it's such an honor and privilege that you would take the time out of your schedule to talk with me. The college is truly fortunate to have an esteemed alumna such as yourself on our side.' "Yvette rolled her eyes. "Do they teach you to talk crap like that?"

I smiled ruefully, nodding. "It's called 'alumni relations.' "

"Alumni relations my ass! Talking to me like I'm three. I'm deaf, not retarded." As if to emphasize this point, she turned up the volume on her hearing aid. "I feel sorry for you, sweetheart. Such a job. Really, I do."

I didn't disagree with her. I'd been yearning to get out for years, but whenever I got close to making a move, it seemed the question of what I'd do instead always got in my way. I didn't want to make a lateral move; I wanted to move in the direction of a passion, something I'd really *enjoy* doing. I just didn't know what that passion was. That was one of the many reasons I enjoyed visiting Yvette: she struck me as just the sort of person who could teach me a thing or two about passion.

I glanced at her out of the corner of my eye, withholding a smirk. "You know, it's not all bad. Sometimes we get to do cool things. Go to special events. The Red Sox occasionally donate tickets. I get to go to a game for free, take alumni along with me. As a goodwill gesture . . . "

Yvette cleared her throat, considering. "Well," she said, after a lengthy pause, her voice taking on a more conciliatory tone, "I suppose it's for a good cause. The college has gotta get money somehow, right? Even if you do hit up little old ladies to do it."

In front of us on the shiny doors of the elevator, our reflections stared as we waited to arrive on Yvette's floor. Looking at the two of us side-by-side made me want to laugh and cry. I was in the dull, professional attire my job required, a smart leather bag I'd received as a graduation gift slung over one shoulder, my hair held up in a French clip. Sometimes, when I got dressed for work in the morning, I couldn't shake the feeling that I was stepping into a cardboard box. Yvette, on the other hand, wore a Red Sox jersey that fit her like a nightgown, coming all the way down to her knees, and a fitted baseball cap that was also too big, hanging jauntily over one eye. I knew underneath that hat was a puff of short gray hair like a bird's nest, something Yvette would have otherwise styled had there not been a game later that evening, a subtle nod to her once pronounced vanity.

She pushed her baseball cap up high on her forehead and looked at me, wringing her hands. "I thought I was going to have a goddamn heart attack today, just thinking about this game."

"Why?"

Yvette gave me a look. "Why, it's the goddamn playoffs, of course! The goddamn playoffs! Tell me: do you or don't you live in Boston?"

The doors opened and she darted out into the hall, leading the way to her room. She'd once told me that she hadn't expected to stay in this place for so long; she'd found being surrounded by old people all the time more than a little depressing. She'd thought the Sox would win it and then she could go join her mother, father, and sister in peace. But it had been over a decade that she'd lived in Sherwood Manor and still no World Series win.

Yvette unlocked the door to her room. Although she acted casual about our visits, I knew that she had been raised properly, in elite private academies, a home of old New England money, and sometimes manners and breeding trumped indifference. "I apologize for the clutter," she said, hurrying to a plate containing the remnants of her early dinner. "They were supposed to have picked this up thirty minutes ago.

Peas!" she declared as she took the plate to the door, leaving it in the hallway. "Goddamn peas! No matter how many times I tell 'em I'm not eating those horrid little things, they still insist on putting them on my plate."

As I stood waiting for Yvette to show me to my seat, I realized that everything of importance to her was here, reduced to a twelve-by-twelve space. "People spend most of their life accumulating stuff," she'd once said, "but at some point you reach a summit of shit and say enough is enough." When her sister passed away, Yvette sold off nearly all of the items that had been saved in her parents' home, then sold the house itself. "It's no good," she'd said, "to worship stuff that way." And yet I knew just from being inside her room that Yvette wasn't above the act of worshiping material possessions.

Little had changed since the last time I was here. Gauzy salmon colored curtains dampened the afternoon light; a small reading lamp next to her bed illuminated the rest. There was still the fold-out chair where I would sit and listen to Yvette tell wistful stories of her youth and complain about Grady Little. There was still the framed picture of Yvette that rested on the black and white television set, taken when she had been in her mid-twenties. In it, Yvette was wearing a sequined ballroom dress with a slit that ran up to mid-thigh, playing tricks on the eye so that it looked as if her five-foot frame had a leg like Ginger Rogers, a cigarette holder clenched suggestively between her teeth. There was still the "No Bullshit" bumper sticker her nephew had bought her years ago taped to the closet door. There was still the poster of Ted Williams, yellow around the edges but in good condition otherwise, the bat about to be let loose from his hands, his body twisted in that moment just after a perfect swing, his eyes focused on a point the rest of us could not see, where the ball has gone sailing out into left field and beyond, out of the ballpark maybe and onto the street. There was still her most prized possession: a baseball signed by Jimmie Foxx that she had inherited from her father, kept in an air-tight glass box; a ball, she'd once told me, that Cooperstown occasionally called and begged her for. Yvette had a knack for hyperbole and I was relatively certain she'd been fibbing about this last detail. But the ball looked so snug in there, so cozy on its velvet throne, that I imagined curling up for a nap inside the box.

As I stood just inside the doorway of Yvette's room, I thought of my studio apartment a couple of miles away. It wasn't much larger than this, but it was so different. I wondered if its contents — the neatly stacked and carefully selected books, my cds organized on a stylish metal rack, the furniture and fishbowl and paintings adorning the walls, the drapes I had put up in an effort to make the space look more like a real home and less like a college dorm — reflected my personality in the way that Yvette's so obviously did. If a stranger were to look in on my space, would they glean information about me from it all?

Something told me I'd be disappointed in the answer to that question. When I thought about Yvette, it seemed more information about her was contained in that autographed baseball she'd inherited from her father than anything else. And try as I might, I couldn't think of a single item I owned that meant as much to me as that ball meant to Yvette.

Yvette followed my gaze and moved to the ball, placing her fingertips gently on the case, an act more of admiration than protectiveness. "They don't make 'em like they used to," she said. "Foxx. That man knew how to hit a baseball. Almost a mockery, the way he died."

I looked at her, waiting, but she seemed to think I should know this information independent of her baseball lessons. "How'd he die?" I finally asked.

"Chicken bone." She sighed. "One of the greatest hitters of all time choked on a chicken bone."

She motioned me to the fold-out chair. I sat down, crossing my legs, waiting for her to pour me a glass of sherry. For decades Yvette had finished each and every one of her dinners with a single Lucky Strike cigarette and a glass of the finest sherry. "My only two vices," she'd said, but then I'd pointed out to her that she had a mouth like a sailor.

"That, my dear girl," she'd replied, "is an asset."

She claimed that the only time she allowed herself seconds on both sherry and cigarettes was when I came to visit. I liked to pretend that in this particular instance, she was telling the truth.

"There's no respect for the game anymore," Yvette continued, going to her dresser where a crystal bottle half-full with sherry rested. Her spoken meanderings were always a mystery to me; sometimes I had the sense that it was all just one long thought and occasionally she'd open her mouth and put sound to it. "Not even Teddy's family. They want to freeze him like a sirloin steak! Can you believe it?"

No, I murmured. I couldn't.

"No respect at all. Teddy wouldn't have approved. I can tell you that much."

According to Yvette, she should've known: she'd once had an affair with Ted Williams, a torrid romance that started during spring training one year and ended just before the playoffs. "Had to dump him before he got too serious; I never was the marrying type." And so she ended it with him just like all the others. And boy oh boy, she'd said, were there others. Bobby Doerr, George Kell, Dom DiMaggio. The names meant nothing to me, except for the last one who I'd mistaken for his brother. But Yvette assured me that each and every one of them had at one time or another been on the Red Sox. The only non-Red Sox player that counted as a notch in her bedpost was Jackie Robinson, and that hadn't been disloyal of her. "It wasn't my fault," she'd said, "that the team was run by a bunch of bigots."

Yvette leaned forward, narrowing her eyes on me. "If it were my decision, Ted's ashes would be spread over Fenway. And not for some bullshit romantic reason, but because those ashes would work magic on that field. *Magic.*"

Always after spending an afternoon with her, I thought this was what it all boiled down to for Yvette: love, death, and baseball.

It was inconceivable to me that Yvette had had an affair with Ted Williams. And yet I couldn't imagine why she would feel compelled to lie to me of all people about a thing like that. It seemed to me that after a certain age, it became ridiculous to say anything other than the absolute truth. And although I didn't know her that well, Yvette struck me as just the sort of person to live by such a dictum.

Today, she was unusually cheery. I knew this when she offered up chocolates and a bag of unshelled peanuts. Sherry was easy to give away;

unshelled peanuts on the other hand, were a gesture of infrequent generosity.

Even though I didn't particularly like them, I broke open a peanut and raised my eyebrows at her. "What's the special occasion?"

Yvette glanced at the clock hanging on her wall, smiling mysteriously. "Well, you're here for one. And then there's this playoff game tonight . . . "

"Do you think we'll win?"

"I don't know, sweetheart. I truly do not know."

Yvette fell into her Lay-Z-Boy chair, stretching out her arms and kicking up her feet. I'd once heard from an aide that worked on Yvette's floor that Yvette put up such a stink about needing to have that particular chair in her room, that the assisted living facility made an exception to its strict policy on medically-approved furniture. Another item that she'd inherited from her father. He'd been forced by Yvette's mother to keep it in his study so that it wouldn't offend the eyes of distinguished guests when they came to visit. It had sat next to the radio where he had listened to the games, and remained there after his death, up until the day that Yvette closed the house for good.

"A part of me thinks we could win," Yvette continued. "But another part of me thinks we're fated to lose. It's this feeling I got in my gut." She pressed her small fist against her round middle. "That Grady Little's no good. Nomar is in trouble. Pedro — an exceptional player but he doesn't know a thing about being gracious. It'll take a miracle for us to win with a team like this. Too many . . . *egos*. Not one cohesive unit." She laced her fingers together to accentuate this point.

I laughed. "Then why keep watching if you think we'll lose?"

Yvette looked at me as if she'd just taken a bite of raw rhubarb. "If I have to explain it to you," she said, her voice low and not a little bit sinister, "you're not worth the time."

"Ouch."

She cracked a peanut with her teeth, tossing the shells on the floor. "You got a boyfriend, darling?"

I blushed, wondering what Yvette might think of me if she knew that unlike herself, I was the dumped, *not* the dumpee. "Nope."

"A girlfriend?"

"*Yvette.*"

"What? You think I haven't been around the block a few times? I was a goddamn flapper for cryin' out loud. We laid the groundwork for girls like you."

I sighed, exasperated. "No girlfriend."

"Too bad. You need a little someone to teach you a thing or two about the Red Sox."

I shrugged. "I never really had that much interest in it. I mean, it's fun and all but-"

She held a finger up, silencing me. "Don't say another word." She glared at the blank screen of the television set and for a moment I thought she might be angry enough to kick me out. But then she smiled softly and turned in my direction. "I suppose we all need someone to teach us a thing or two in life.

Did you know I have season tickets?"

"Season tickets?"

"At Fenway! My father left them to me." She tucked a small curl that had escaped out from under her hat back in, an act so striking that for a moment I could imagine her as that woman in the picture frame, that young flapper at the parties, drinking martinis and smoking cigarettes, telling dirty jokes, pressing herself close to the men and women she knew adored her. "Dad would have appreciated Nomar. Varitek. The more cerebral, misunderstood types. Me, I just like a meathead who can hit."

"Aren't they all meatheads?"

"Are you looking to leave early today?"

I laughed. The sherry had gone straight to my head. "Okay, okay. So what happened to the tickets?"

"Ah, those. My nephew uses them. Honestly, I don't think he treats them with the respect they deserve. Takes his business associates to the games; the rest of the time charges his friends and acquaintances for them. But he's my only family left."

"Is he cute? Maybe he can teach me a thing or two about the Red Sox."

"Nah, he's not your type."

"What's my type?"

Yvette paused, looking off at some invisible point on the wall. She placed her hand on her chest. "Well...a male version of me."

In a sense, she was right. I loved to visit Yvette because she was my favorite sort of person: vivid, original. A person that sometimes scared me, sometimes made me sad, always made me laugh. A person I frequently aspired to be.

I leaned closer to Yvette and placed my hand gently on her arm. "Then maybe you can teach me a thing or two about the Red Sox."

Yvette met my gaze. Her hazel eyes had gone all liquid but I couldn't find a single tear in them. "Maybe you're right. Maybe I can."

That night, Thursday, October 16th, the Red Sox lost to the Yankees, ending their playoff run in the 2003 season.

But when I called Yvette to send my condolences, she was shockingly upbeat.

"That was one hell of a home run Aaron Boone hit!" she declared, her voice filled with genuine admiration.

"But Yvette! They *lost!*"

"Exactly. Imagine what would happen if we'd won? Or worse still, if we won the World Series? The Nation would have nothing left. Losing means we'll just have to keep on hoping. And that's what it's all about: another season of hope."

"Another season of hope?" I echoed.

"Yep. You don't have much in life if you don't have that."

After hanging up the telephone, I puzzled over Yvette. She claimed that any other person who was a Red Sox fan would understand, but I couldn't help but feel that it was something special to do with her. My suspicions were strengthened later in the day when I learned that two of the men who worked in the printing office had both called into work sick.

"Sick to death," one of their colleagues said, his mouth curling in a sneer as he handed over a stack of newsletters I'd had printed for our office. When I didn't respond, he looked at me more closely. "They're both diehard Sox fans."

It takes hard work to avoid the Red Sox when you live in Boston. But the disappointments of 2003 were too much to ignore, and so in the weeks and months that followed, I relented. I watched on with the rest of the Nation as Grady Little was fired, speculated with friends and colleagues over whether or not Nomar would stay, debated Manny's loyalty when he arrived late to spring training. I collected so much information about who had been at fault and what had gone wrong, that I felt my confidence boosted by increased Red Sox knowledge and became eager to visit Yvette again. I felt I'd finally have something to contribute to our visits, something to offer her, and in some small way, redeem myself.

I hadn't anticipated that Yvette was one step ahead of me.

I'd just opened my calendar one morning at work to set up a date when the telephone rang. Spring training was ending in a week; the official 2004 baseball season was just about to begin. Signs of it were everywhere — stores were stocking up with red and blue T-shirts, kids braved the still wintry temperatures to run around frozen baseball diamonds, a donut chain displayed cardboard cutouts of Johnny Damon at all of its Boston-area locations, a furniture company's commercials spotlighted Tim Wakefield. I wondered just before picking up the receiver if it wasn't Yvette herself, calling to ask me if I'd learned a thing or two since last we'd seen each other, wondering if I knew what time of year it truly was. I wanted to impress her by opening our discussion with a question that would make her swoon: what did she think of this new guy Schilling?

But instead, the person on the other end of the line told me that he was an attorney from a law firm downtown, and that he was responsible for managing the estate of Yvette Bouchard.

"Yvette?" I echoed. Something about his tone stopped me from saying more.

"That's correct. I'm not sure if you're aware, but she passed away two weeks ago. Her nephew is her only remaining living family member, and he and I have been going over her estate together. She had detailed some special requests."

Salt clotted my throat. I wondered how Barbara — how I — had missed this bit of information. It seemed somehow I should have known. "I'm sorry. Yvette, she's ... dead?"

"It happened peacefully, in her sleep." The attorney paused. "You knew her."

It was a statement, not a question.

"No, Yes. I mean, not well." Disappointment was quickly washed away by regret and then genuine sorrow, filling up my chest, flood waters rising in a shallow basement.

The attorney chuckled. "You knew her well enough."

I rubbed at one eye with the heel of my free hand. "Is this about her leaving a gift?"

"Yes. Yes it is."

"Well, you'll need to talk to my boss, Barbara Stevenson. She's the one who handles endowments. I just assist her with individual dona-tions."

"This isn't an endowment. This is a personal gift. To you."

He explained to me that on October 17th, 2003, the day after I'd last seen her, the day after the Red Sox lost in the playoffs to the Yankees, Yvette had visited him at his office and made changes in her final will and testimony. Those changes included giving me her season tickets. They also included the baseball signed by Jimmie Foxx.

"I don't understand," I said. "Why would she leave those to me?"

"She said she thought you'd appreciate them."

After work, I went to the law offices to sign some papers and pick up the baseball. It looked incongruous, bedded in its glass box, perched on a tall stack of legal documents. I wondered if the attorney had any idea about the ball, knew anything about Jimmie Foxx, but my musings were interrupted when he said: "The Baseball Hall of Fame has already called about that ball. I imagine they'd be willing to put in an offer. Appears Mr. Foxx didn't sign many of those in his lifetime. He hit a home run with that particular ball, helped the team win an important game."

I tucked the box inside my jacket, pressing it close to me on the subway ride home, the pointy corners digging under my ribcage. I spent most of the night laying flat on my back in bed, holding the box up to the light, inspecting the carefully sewn seams of the ball, the scribble of Jimmie Foxx's signature, some illegible note that Yvette had once claimed read: "From one fox to another" until I had pointed out to her that it had first been given not to Yvette, but to her father. I smiled then, to think of her giggling and blushing, caught in the act, pouring herself a second glass of sherry, winking at me before taking a long sip. "Nothing gets past you, does it?" she'd said.

What would I do with those tickets? With that ball? The only answer I could come up with seemed unfair, highway robbery, really. But it also seemed like the only conclusion to an unlikely friendship: attend every game possible.

The 2004 season would be my initiation into Red Sox Nation. I considered inviting a friend or family member to the opener at Fenway; it wouldn't have been hard to find someone. But after thinking about it, the only person I could imagine joining me for that particular game was the same person who'd gotten me to Fenway Park in the first place.

I decided to go alone.

Fantasy Camp: A Satire

TIMOTHY GAGER

For The Renegades and George Plimpton, the father of fantasy athletics.

AUGUST 2005, THE DARE

Today my softball season ends. We are the league champs. I've played on this team for fifteen years and we've never won anything. If we even made the playoffs we would be the last team in, slotted against the top seed and bounced in the first round. This year we win, pour beer over each other's heads, have a group hug, and then, ten minutes later, look at each other and ask, "What's next?" My buddy Jon McPhail walks over and says, "Red Sox Fantasy Camp, next February. We should go." We fit the requirement: a little over weight and over forty. Feeling my championship bravado, I say, "I'm in."

DECEMBER 2005, THE TRUTH

Jon calls and I have to tell him. I don't have to lie, just speak the truth. "Jon, I'm fifty years old, my son is about to enter college, and I really don't have the $3700 to go to the camp. Sorry to disappoint you."

"You mean I signed up and have to do this alone?"

"No, I'll be there, but not with the Red Sox camp." There is a pause on the other end. I expect it. "I signed up for Red Sox Fantasy Reporter Camp. It is only $500 and I get to write about the camp. It's like being a sports reporter for a week. I'll have access to all the players."

"Will you be in the same hotel as us?"

"Well, the way it was put to me was that I had to pay that bill myself. I'm staying at the Super 8 in Fort Myers. Twenty-nine ninety-nine a night."

"According to the brochure, we'll have 'deluxe accommodations' at the Red Sox camp," McPhail gloats.

"Is there a curfew?"

"Yes, just like the bigs. Hey, it says McNamara's running the squad."

"No shit?"

"No shit."

"He'll be doing the bed checks, no doubt."

"Ain't that a gas?"

FEBRUARY 5, 2006, 10:00 A.M., ALMOST PERFECTION

The grass is green, as green as it should be, and at the same time more color than can be digested. The dirt, glowing burnt clay. The balls, bleached, white, arching across the endless blue sky. The uniforms, red, and bright enough to make one fear a direct look. Still, there is something wrong with this picture. Missed throws bounce across the field. The crack of the bat is more like a splat than the thunderclap of a professional. The team is old, lumpy, wearing the numbers of Manny Ramirez, Curt Schilling, and Carlton Fisk, but looking more like Paul Williams than Ted. They've all paid top dollar for this dream of re-living their youths, experiencing the big 'what if,' even if that 'what if' was never even close.

The group is broken into several squads, each led by an ex-ballplayer. I recognize Jim Willoughby working with the pitchers, Jim Rice at the batting cage, and Bill Buckner around the bag at first. When a ground ball goes through the legs of one of the campers, no one wants to look at Buckner except me. I notice him rolling his eyes. He glares right at me, more flushed than the team's red jerseys. "Hey," he barks. "Reporter."

"Me?"

"No, the other hundred Fantasy Reporters." The squad laughs.

"Mac wants to see you. Be in the hotel lobby tonight, 10:30."

"Thanks," I say.

"Now catch that damn thing," he yells to the camper. "Christ, how can you miss something like that?"

FEBRUARY 5, 2006, 10:45 P.M., THE GHOST

I am late. He sits, waiting, a lone figure in the lobby bar. He is more grey and wrinkled than I remember, but 1986 is long ago. His plaid button-down shirt is neat, pressed, but still a relic from that era. I stick out my hand. "Thanks for the invitation," I say.

"Well, there should always be a good drinking relationship between the press and the coaches."

"Speaking of which, where are your coaches? Don't you usually have a few you hire to hang out with in the lobby?"

He scratches his head. "Well, it's harder after '86. Must be a guilt by association thing. I spend lots of evenings exactly like this." He sips from a white creamy drink with ice. Funny that I'd pictured him as a bourbon man.

"White Russian?" I ask, pointing to his glass.

"Fuck no. It's Ensure. It's all I drink now. It has vitamins and food products all in one. Try some."

"No thanks," I say, trying to get back to business. "Look, I need to write an article on the camp and I was hoping you'd help me out." I always have problems being blunt, but I came to Florida with a goal and I am not about to let my inhibitions stop me.

"I guess you want to talk about 1986." His hand tightens around his glass and he picks it up to drink. "First of all, I was Manager of the Year that year and all they want to remember is that one play. The fact is that people are ignorant. Most people think the Buckner play ended the World Series. In fact, that play wasn't the final play of the Series, it was only Game Six! There was another game, but no one remembers it!" Mc-Namara slams down his glass and some Ensure slops over the lip onto the table. His nose has turned red. "And Stapelton at first? I hardly used him there all season. No one remembers that either. What I really meant to do in Game Six was have Stapelton catch. But I decided Gedman deserved to be in there for the clincher. No one gave me credit for that! No! Gedman played a perfect final inning and no one gave me any credit."

"Actually, John, I just wanted to talk about this year's camp."

"Oh, that. Well, we have a wonderful camp. The squads look good, and each year they come in better and better shape. Except that Mc-Phail. I have my eye on him. I think he's out missing curfew."

"Couldn't talk any of the coaches into this gig tonight? Pesky? Harper?"

"Gig?" He gives me one of those "these young people today" looks.

"I mean job. Sorry."

"As I said before, it's tough to get the coaches to join me. Except maybe Billy."

"Billy?" I am not aware of any coach named Billy on the fantasy roster this year.

"Billy Martin," he adds.

"Didn't he . . . "

"Wrap his car around a tree? Yes, but I'm talking about his ghost."

"His ghost?"

"Billy's ghost drinks at every hotel lobby in the major leagues. He's been here. Actually, it's comforting to have him here, until he has too many and wants to fight. Sometimes he throws glasses."

"Really?" I'm having a tough time imagining the ghost of Billy the Kid involved in a paranormal phenomenon, hurling glasses and such.

"Yes. At one point they hired a company called Mystery Inc. to look into it. It turned out that they were just a bunch of meddling kids."

"John, I think perhaps you're . . . " The front door of the lobby opens, interrupts me.

"HEY YOU," McNamara stands and shouts to Jon McPhail who is returning with a woman on each arm. "You're fined for missing curfew. The court will see you tomorrow." McPhail shrugs his shoulders, jumps on the elevator.

"What were we talking about?" McNamara asks.

"Oh, I forget," I lie. "Getting kind of late for me. Should head on back and turn in."

"I'll be here for a few more." He points at his Ensure. "Good night."

FEBRUARY 6, 2006, 3:00 P.M., KANGAROO COURT

There is an announcement in the locker room after today's intersquad games. "Court's in session, the honorable Don Baylor presiding. First case is the Red Sox versus Ryan Cambello." The room grows loud. "Ryan, you are being charged with failure to cover first base on a ground ball. That will cost you twenty-five bucks. How do you plead?"

"What's this about?" Cambello asks.

"It's a Major League tradition used to raise money for some event or charity. Players are fined based on poor execution of fundamentals or anything else the court deems worthy," Lee Gasser replies.

"Thanks for the explanation," Baylor says. "Stand up, son."

"I am standing." Gasser has no legs.

"Oh sorry," Baylor pauses. "Court fines you twenty dollars for non-compliance of an official order. How do you play, son?"

"Guilty, I guess," Gasser says.

"Not plead, play. You have no legs."

"Oh, I use the artificial ones then."

"Good," Baylor says. "So you're guilty of not standing then. How about you, Cambello?"

"Guilty."

"Twenty-five bucks. See the clerk on the way out. Next case, the Red Sox versus Jon McPhail. Jon you are charged for missing curfew and bringing two women into the hotel. One hundred dollar fine! Your plea?"

"Not guilty," McPhail pleads.

"Not guilty? McNamara and a reporter both saw you."

"Well, I may be guilty of being late on the curfew, but I can't be found guilty for the two ladies."

"Well why is that?"

"They were from another camp."

"Another camp?" Baylor laughs. "Do the Twins have women this year?"

"No," McPhail answers. "They are from the Baseball Annie Fantasy Camp. They are older women who never went with ballplayers when they were young. At this camp they pay to go after the Fantasy Ballplayers in our camps. It's new."

"So let me get this straight. They pay to be groupies?" Baylor scratches his chin.

"Kind of," McPhail answers. "They're paying more for the dream of being something that they're not. Kind of like what we're doing."

"Huh," Baylor says. He looks perplexed. "Twenty-five for missing curfew and twenty-five back to each of the girls. You aren't worth paying for. Next case!"

FEBRUARY 7, 2006, 11:30 A.M., UMPIRE FANTASY CAMP
The routine here is fairly regimented. Work-outs in the morning, lunch at noon, and games between the squads in the afternoon. The week culminates with an umpired game pitting the ex-players against the campers, to be held at City of Palms Park, the actual stadium where the real Red Sox play. The umpires will be from the Fantasy Umpire Camp held down the street and run by former major league umpire Al Clark. I've been at the Red Sox camp for two days so I decide a change of scenery might be good.

Al Clark's camp is held at Fort Myers High School. As I pull up there seems to be a large assembly of men and women in blue suits playing "Simon Says." I recognize Al immediately. He had been on Court TV recently, guilty of fraud for selling fake "game-used" balls that hadn't been. Al is in front of the group, demonstrating the familiar arm signals while shouting "OUT" and "SAFE" as the eager umpires in training repeat every gesture.

"OUT!"

"OUT!" yells the group.

"SAFE!"

"SAFE!"

"OK, enough of that," Clark relaxes.

"OK, enough of that," the group replies. Clark stops talking for a minute as the squad regroups.

"What I want to go over now is how to handle an argument. I mean, we all argue, but part of the baseball argument is the explanation of what you viewed on the field. Are you following me so far?"

"SAFE!" shouts the group.

"Good. Now when it goes too far, managers and players can say some pretty rough things. So what I want to do is role-play. Carter, come up here." Carter is a wiry man who looks like a librarian. "Let's see how you handle this." Clark takes a deep breath, moves his face within inches of Carter's and wails, "I CAN'T BELIEVE YOU DIDN'T SEE THAT! DO YOU NEED GLASSES OR SOMETHING!"

Carter takes a step back, looks befuddled.

"Well?" Clark asks. "What?"

"I can't believe you didn't see that. Do you need glasses or something?" Carter responds.

"Carter, it's not time to repeat now."

"Sorry."

"So what will you do when a manager gets in your face and says, I CAN'T BELIEVE YOU DIDN'T SEE THAT! DO YOU NEED GLASSES OR SOMETHING!"

"I'll say OK,"

"OK?"

"Yes. I do need a new prescription. Know any good ophthalmologists in Fort Myers?" Clark lets out a slight groan. "Anybody else?"

Half the umpires say "SAFE" and the others yell out "BALL." Clark looks down at his black umpire shoes. "Maybe we should go back to the basics. Everyone ready?"

"YES," yell the group.

"OUT!"

"OUT!"

"SAFE!"

"SAFE!"

"Yerrrrrrrrr OUT!"

"Yerrrrrrrrr OUT!"

"STEAR-IKE"

"STRIKE!"

FEBRUARY 7, 2006, 1:00 P.M., THROWING OUT YOUR LEG
McPhail finds me during a break and says, "I've heard of throwing out your arm, but Gasser is the first ballplayer to ever throw out his leg." Indeed, Gasser has forgone use of his artificial legs this morning and is

leading off the intersquad game without them. He is no bigger than three and a half feet tall on his stumps and Cambello is having a tough time throwing him a strike. "Hey, he can't do that," Cambello complains after missing the tiny strike zone three times in a row.

"The Americans with Disabilities Act states that as a disabled adult I must be allowed to do the things the non-disabled can do. Concessions must be made if I cannot do so. So shove it up your ass."

"Stick it in his ear," former Red Sox pitching coach John Cumberland shouts. And he does. Cambello fires a pitch off Gasser's batting helmet.

"Hey, mother-fucker," Gasser yells.

"What you going to do? Charge the mound?"

Tommy Harper steps in. "Come on boys, we're here to have fun. Take your base, Gasser." Gasser slowly inches his way toward first by his stumps.

"Tom Mitchell, Run for Gasser," Harper orders.

"Ooooh, no," Gasser chides. "I paid good money to participate and I'm going to run for myself. Remember what the America for Disabilities Act says. It says. . . ." Some of the campers take the moment to sit in the grass. "If he keeps this up," Mitchell says to McPhail, "The game will last till tomorrow."

"If he keeps this up, I'm going to use the little bastard for a hitting tee."

FEBRUARY 8, 2006, 5:00 P.M., DINING HALL

Tonight's meal is steak, mashed potatoes and corn on the cob. McPhail is rowing the corn around in his hands while eating and smacking his lips. "Ummm-huh," he lets out. "Nothing like an all-you-can-eat to pack on the pounds." The players get their meals as part of the camp; mine costs $13.75. I use a credit card. "You should eat leftovers off Gasser's plate," McPhail tells me. "They're getting a deal on him."

"I'm surprised he hasn't sued the place because of it."

I don't realize that Gasser is sitting at the table directly behind us. "You're pretty fucking funny," he turns and says. "I suppose in your spare time you like to make fun of burn victims, too."

"Look, I'm sorry. I didn't realize you were there. I'm just learning things, you know, trying to be observant as a reporter."

"They should throw you off that paper."

"You available for an interview?" I ask.

"After what you wrote yesterday about how slow I am, I'm not talking to the press."

"Well, I really am not in the press per se."

"I'm not going to talk to you at all then." Gasser scoops up some mashed potatoes on his spoon, reels it back like a catapult and launches it against the side of my head. It hits with a large thud, then deflects onto my pants and shoulders. "Deion Sanders was right," he says. Gasser stands up with his tray; his distinctive laugh carries over everyone else's.

FEBRUARY 9, 2006, 10:00 A.M., LEE

Bill Lee arrives today, distracting the others from my humiliation. The first thing he wants to know is if Don Zimmer is here. "Where is he?" he shouts. "Where is Zimmer?" Lee has some local kid driving a golf cart, trailing him wherever he goes. In the back is a fifty-pound bag of wood chips marked "bedding for gerbils." "Hey, is that for Zimmer?" Bob Stanley yells. "He's not here this year."

"I know, but that's my cover. I get a lot of mileage out of that Zimmer joke," Lee says reaching into the middle of the chips and pulling a large bag of reefer. "Hard to transport this stuff from Vermont without drawing undue attention. Who said Zim never helped me?" he laughs.

"Great," Stanley adds. "Now management is going to keep a tight eye on us."

"What are you worried about?" Lee fires back, rolling a joint. "If you're not getting caught, you have no reason to be concerned."

FEBRUARY 9, 2006, 2:00 P.M., NUTRITION

This afternoon Gasser launches a 400 foot home run followed by another deep long ball from lanky camper Tom Mitchell. The opposing pitcher, Jim Lonborg, looks perplexed. "This camp is showing me something," he says. "Those balls were only going 250 yesterday."

"Think it's the balls?" McNamara asks.

"Well, I don't know."

Cambello tells me that yesterday there was an unauthorized trainer at the camp site. He thinks Gasser and Mitchell were working out with him.

"Yeah, I saw him too." I say. "He didn't look like a trainer. Did he seem kind of big?"

"Yeah that's him. His name was Alexander or something."

"Yeah, I tried to talk to him, but he declined an interview. He did tell me that he works for a nutritional supplement company."

"Yeah, Mr. Reporter, you seem to get a lot of those. Why do you think people won't talk to you?" Cambello asks.

"I don't know. Beats me."

"Well, you can't use any of what we are talking about now either. It is off the record."

"Fine. So you did talk to him?"

"Yes."

"And you said his name was Alexander?"

"Yes."

"That's funny. I thought his name was Manny. I have a lot to learn." I am startled by another loud crack as Gasser clears the fences again. He circles the bases, taking only a few seconds this time, still running on his oversized stumps.

FEBRUARY 10, 2006, 10:30 A.M., CUP CHECK

Camp is shut down this morning as team doctors perform urine tests on all the players and coaches. McPhail says Gasser will grant me an interview if I switch my urine for his. I decline.

"Imagine that," McPhail adds. "They're checking for steroids, greenies and human growth hormones. They say even here it's a black eye for baseball."

"What about Manny Alexander?"

"He was asked to leave camp. I think there's a story in there, if you can find him."

"As long as camp is shut down I'll try to find McNamara and get the scoop."

As I walk through the campus to the main field, I find some of the players milling around. "Good day for baseball," I say to one, fully knowing that there are no scrimmages or practice until all test results come back. "Let's hope so," someone answers. "If you're looking for Skip, you'd better hurry. He's packing up his things."

FEBRUARY 10, 2006, 10:40 A.M., MANAGER'S OFFICE

McNamara is filling a cardboard box with belongings when I walk in. "Can you believe this shit?" he asks. His face is slow and sad.

"I heard. Did it have to do with the steroids?"

"No, some meeting. It was the damndest thing." McNamara says, shaking his head. He is loading the box with pens, pencils, sunflower seeds, and handfuls of other snacks. "I get called into Duquette's office. Now I've never met the man, but he introduces me to another guy... some kid." McNamara shakes his head, his face beginning to turn red. "And this kid says, 'Mr. Kennedy...' Can you imagine? This kid thought I was Kevin Kennedy. Imagine that? So anyway, Duquette corrects him and he's all embarrassed and apologizes to me. The kid says he's a big fan and what a great manager I am and then he says, 'What I meant was, Mr. McNamara, you're fired!'"

"Fired?"

"Yes, fired! Then this snot nose kid turns to Duquette and says, 'So, how did I do?' Duquette's giving him feedback and shit, then he wants the kid to do it again with a firmer voice. 'No wavering,' Duquette says and he asks me if I could turn around and enter the office again. They wanted to do it again!"

"Really? Ha."

"Ha? It may seem funny to you, but it isn't to me. I'm the one that's been fired before. Many times. I never thought I'd have to deal with it again... and twice for that matter." He turns to face me and I see he's starting to cry. My heart sinks and I feel empathy toward this man.

"Well I'm, sorry to hear that John," I say, seeing all the years of managerial disappointments on his face. "You're a good man, a good baseball man. Something will come along, it always does."

"Well there are always the Padres or the Cubs. They have camps too; they may want to give me another chance."

"I hope so. Thanks for the time you gave to the press. Even if it was only a few days, I appreciate it." Behind his desk I see cases of Ensure stacked up on a metal dolly.

"Good luck," he says while dumping the contents of the center desk drawer into another box. "You're right; I'm sure something will come along. It always does."

FEBRUARY 12, 2006, 1:05 P.M., PRESS BOX

The camp moves to City of Palms Park for the final game. It pits the fantasy players against the ex-Sox in front of a packed house. I settle into the press box, which is loaded for comfort, with high-backed leather seats, silver metal desks, a full refrigerator and a row of brand-new computers. For my final column, I've been told to keep it soft, no critical comments. My previous writing has been shredded by the camp's editor; the final products end up as puff pieces after Gasser threatens the publisher with a lawsuit. Gasser is no longer here, leaving after the steroid scandal with a new pending lawsuit, claiming discrimination against the camp, the Red Sox and Manny Alexander.

The game itself is fairly entertaining, with the campers and the ex-players doing better than expected. Bill Lee looks dominating, striking out the side, much to the complaints of McPhail and the boys. On the other side, Cambello gives up hits to the first four men he faces, but manages to get two outs as Wendell Kim, the third-base coach, tries to wave them home on short balls to left. When Gedman whiffs, Cambello is out of the jam.

From up in the box, the game moves slower than in the big leagues. Players can masquerade from home to first, but trying to take an extra-base or cut off a ball in the gap is like an automobile on its last mile. Conversely, the umpires from Clark's school are difficult to discriminate from any you might see at any major league park; blending into the game, loudly announcing their calls, and gesturing with the proper amount of exaggeration. The biggest jolt of reality is when the game halts with the snap of McPhail's collarbone after a collision at home plate. "HE'S OUT," umpire Carter wails, his glasses falling off his face from the force of his enthusiasm. The medical staff gather round and lift

McPhail out on a stretcher as the capacity crowd, who have paid nothing, give him a standing ovation.

Later, when I see him in the runway, he is gloating. "Did you hear them? Did you hear them cheering? This is why we came here, pal; this is what it's about." When I write it up, I give him the heroic wounded soldier treatment, prose that would have made Ernie Pyle proud.

FEBRUARY 12, 2006, 4:35 P.M., THE LOCKER ROOM

The game is done and the players are packing up, not just from the day but from the week. The ex-players defeat the campers 8-1, their only run coming home on a wild pitch from Matt Young. In the losing locker room, many of the campers clap hugs on each other and shake hands. They bid their farewells to their teammates and to the former Red Sox players who have worked the camp. I catch the eye of Joe Morgan, McNamara's replacement, who says to me, "Six, one and even. That's how it all goes."

"Isn't it six, two and even?"

"Listen, son, it's my phrase and if you've been around as long as I have, it's anything I want it to be." He looks a little frustrated when he says it. "Besides, it doesn't make any sense to begin with." Someone taps him on the shoulder. "Joe. Do you mind heading up to Mr. Duquette's office. Someone up there wants to talk to you." Morgan shakes his head. "Well, there's still some snow expected in Walpole. I'll always have something to do."

McPhail walks back to the locker room, arm to chest in a sling. The players gather round him, exchanging stories, re-living the play where he was hurt. "I'll be back," he says.

"Back?"

"Thing is, Tim," he tells me. "Next year is free. Because of this injury I can come back next year all expenses paid. Do you want to come back?"

Feeling my press credential bravado, I smile and say, "I'm in."

Johnny Boy

MITCH EVICH

Luke Stadleman's wife, Leslie, tells him that they are lucky he was a failure. She says she never would have been attracted to a baseball star. To which Luke, 35 years old and the best centerfielder the North Shore Men's Slow-Pitch League has ever seen, replies, "If I'd been a star you'd have never met me. You wouldn't have got near me."

"True," Leslie replies, sipping from a mug of green tea and surveying the disaster that is their living room, plastic fruits and vegetables all over the place and dolls abandoned in positions that make them look injured. "You probably would have ended up marrying some vapid model, just like Johnny Damon did."

"And I'd be totally miserable," Luke says.

"You bet. You'd be questioning what it all meant — fame and money and beautiful stupid women."

Luke takes a swallow of coffee, which tastes burnt from the extra hour it spent on the hot pad this morning before he finally got out of bed. It's a Saturday and the girls are on the couch in their pajamas, mesmerized by a Clifford video they know by heart. He thumbs through the sports section of the Boston Globe, sees that Johnny Boy is mouthing off again, still can't get over the rude reception from the fans at Fenway earlier in the week. What did he expect? As Leslie put it, back when his defection to the Yankees was announced, "He's doing to *us* the same thing he did to his first wife." Yes, Luke thinks now, and Damon probably doesn't understand why *she's* angry at him, too.

But he decides not to disclose this insight to Leslie because he does not want to spend the next half-hour talking about it. One of the pleasant surprises about Leslie when they met, a decade ago, was that she had zero interest in baseball. Luke had washed out of the minors by then and signed on for a season in an independent league with the Elmira Pioneers — a team consisting largely of players who had not yet learned to read the writing on the wall. There were stories of guys being discovered by major league scouts while hitting the crap out of the ball, but the stories were like the ones you hear about someone winning the lottery in your town. If anything, they made your own odds seem more remote. It was during the seven-hour bus ride, from Elmira to Lynn, a squeaky windshield wiper making it impossible for him to sleep, that Luke concluded his chances were zilch.

That night, at old Fraser Field against the Massachusetts Mad Dogs, Luke went 3 for 4 with two doubles and a stolen base, and the old feeling came back, that this was what he was put on earth to do. Yet the next afternoon, not long before he was due to report for batting practice, there he was at the Lynn Public Library, trying to find the Career Help section.

Leslie was the librarian, and Luke remembers thinking that she looked the part: auburn hair knotted in back, unfashionable glasses with large round lenses. Though she did not actually take him by the hand and lead him to what he was looking for, it now seems as if she did. In the hushed tone required by the surroundings, she asked what Luke's background was.

"My background?"

"The kind of jobs you've done. Your education."

"I graduated from high school. Does that help?"

"It means you don't have to go back and get your G.E.D. What kind of work have you been doing?"

"I'm a baseball player," Luke said, which must have sounded the same to Leslie as if he'd proclaimed himself a Boy Scout." I play for a team from Elmira, New York. We're in town to play the Mad Dogs."

"The Mad Dogs?" There was an arching of eyebrows and a mild, unreadable smile.

"The team that plays at Fraser Field."

"I see," Leslie replied, though she showed no indication of recognizing the stadium's name. "And you're tired of playing baseball now. You want to do something else."

"It's not that I'm tired — "

She raised a finger as if to shush him, and Luke said, in a much quieter voice, "Sorry. It's not that I'm tired of playing baseball. It's just..."

What he had tried to say, but couldn't, was that he wasn't a good enough ballplayer to make a living at it. He couldn't say this because he wasn't sure it was true. But he also couldn't say it because it might be true. He didn't know.

"It's just that I have to quit. I can feel it right here, in my gut," he said, tapping two fingers against his abdominal muscles. "It's not working out." He lowered his head, wanting her pity but not wanting much of it. If there was too much he would put on his swagger mask, the one he wore in the batter's box. He would brusquely thank her for her help and leave.

"It's always hard to change course," she said matter-of-factly. "So you've been playing baseball professionally ever since you graduated from high school?"

Luke explained how he'd been chosen by the Toronto Blue Jays in the third round of the 1990 draft. But he also had to explain how the draft worked, and why a team from Toronto played in the American League. He told her about Dunedin, Florida, and Syracuse, and how, just before the players' strike in 1994, he made his major league debut against the Yankees, in Yankee Stadium, and waited for her to be impressed. Then he asked her, in too loud a voice, if she'd meet him for a drink after tonight's game.

An elderly gentleman looked up from the newspaper he was reading as Leslie gazed back at him with the slightest of smiles while Luke waited, anxiously, for her reply.

Everyone in North Reading, the town where Leslie grew up and where Luke now works as parks and recreation director, assumes that Luke must be a huge baseball fan, having played professional ball himself. In the spring he receives a small additional stipend from the high school for his work as "special instructor" to the baseball team. His duties, as described in the contract he received, involve "providing technical advice on hitting, fielding and other aspects of baseball," but Luke is also expected to regale the lads — and, for that matter, the coaching staff — with stories from his playing days. Of particular interest are the future stars whose paths crossed Luke's in the minor leagues, and the most popular story of all concerns the time that Luke, having been released by the Blue Jays and picked up by the Colorado Rockies, found himself in Wichita, Kansas, playing for the Tulsa Drillers against a team whose lead-off hitter was a hot-hitting 21-year-old named Johnny Damon.

What makes the story rich is that Luke and Damon were similar prospects — slender left-handed hitting outfielders with excellent speed and reputations for recklessly pursuing fly balls. (Though Stadleman had a better throwing arm.) On this particular night in Wichita, however, Damon was hitting close to .350. Within a week, he would join the Kansas City Royals and never play in the minor leagues again. Stadleman, who hated Tulsa as much as any player has ever hated any place, would find himself a year later in the reference section of the Lynn Public Library, unable to stop thinking about the librarian who had agreed to meet him that night for a drink.

But all those things were in the future. That night the wind blew hot off the prairie, curling the American flag high above the centerfield fence and causing fly balls to flutter like kites. In the first inning, Luke staggered toward what should have been a routine out and lost his hat as he tumbled, the ball lodged in the crease of his glove. The crowd sighed in disappointment as he got to his knees and held the ball aloft. As he trotted back towards where he would position himself for the next batter, a gust of wind carried an odor that was almost putrid, fertilizer or stockyards, Luke wasn't sure which.

At bat the prairie wind was Luke's friend. Damon couldn't reach a ball that got up against the wall in right center, and Luke took advantage of Damon's girlish way of throwing and beat the relay throw for a triple.

Two innings later Damon was at the wall again, but this time he didn't even bother to leap. Luke's shot disappeared into the dark, and as he rounded the bases, he heard the public address guy announce, in a muted voice, "Home run — Luke Stadleman." The final score was 5-4, the final out recorded when Luke, his back to home plate and the wind in his ears, made an over-the-shoulder catch on the warning track, turning just in time so that his shoulders absorbed the force of his body slamming backwards against the wall.

Luke gets tired of telling this story, but it is what people want to hear. He never talks about what happened at Yankee Stadium.

"So what time's your softball game today?" Leslie says from the living room, where the Clifford video has ended and the girls are demanding that they be allowed to watch it again. Katie's lower lip is quivering, and big-girl Jill gazes at her mom in a way that makes her look like a miniature teenager, arms folded against her belly and staring at the rug.

"Two games, actually. The first one starts at one o'clock."

"So I'll be alone with these two all afternoon."

"Why not bring them along to watch? I think the field we're playing at has a playground near it. It would be good for them to see what their dad actually does."

"You make it sound like that's how you support the family," Leslie says.

"You know what I mean," Luke replies, but in fact he's not quite sure. He feels like a guy in Springsteen's song "Glory Days," always telling boring stories no one wants to hear. Leslie has informed him the song is a real crowd-pleaser between innings at Fenway, thanks to its raucous chorus. Luke wouldn't know; he hasn't been to the ballpark since back when you could drive in on the day of the game and still buy tickets.

"And then next week is that tournament, and you'll be gone for the whole weekend."

The statement is part lament, part question. Luke says, "Yes, I'll be gone for the whole weekend, including Friday. I'm going to have some fun for a change."

"So will I," Leslie replies. "I'll leave the girls to fend for themselves, and I'll go off drinking and dancing with my friends."

"Why not get your dad to watch them?"

"Wrong generation, Luke. He'd just sit them down in front of the TV all night."

"Is that the worse thing in the world?"

Leslie gives him her librarian stare, a pursing of her lips and a narrowing of her eyes. "They watch too much as it is, the days when you're the one who's home alone."

Which is each Monday, ever since Town Meeting, following the recommendation of the board of selectmen, voted to reduce Luke's hours as a cost-saving measure. Leslie's dad, Stan Hinsdale, has been a selectman ever since Leslie was in high school, and in this case discreetely recused himself from the vote. Stan Hinsdale, as everyone knows, is the reason Luke was given the parks and rec job in the first place. In every other town, the person who holds this job has a college degree.

Luke sat quietly through the Town Meeting discussion, as several people rose to say nice things about him before recommending that his salary be reduced by 20 percent.

"OK, I'm sorry. I won't go to Syracuse next weekend. It's not like my teammates are counting on me. I mean, I'm sure they can find someone else who can play center field every bit as well as I can, and can hit for power, and go from first to home on a hit to the outfield. It's not like any of us are interested in *winning*. If my absence costs us the chance to become tournament champions, none of the guys will mind. We're just out to have fun."

Leslie rolls her eyes, and Luke wishes he had stopped about four sentences earlier. The scary thing is how much these games matter to him. It's *softball,* after all, they might as well be putting the ball on a goddamned tee. The gossip around town is that Luke is under the delusion that some major league scout is going to see him tearing up the local slow-pitch league and invite him for a try-out. Just like in that movie about the 37-year-old pitcher.

Luke, as Leslie knows, is not delusional. But when the ball is hit over his head something kicks in that he can't really control. Last season he came home one night with a gash across his cheek and swelling on his knee, courtesy of the galvanized fence he collided with. But the important thing, he said, (he really said this) "is that I managed to hang on to the ball. Two runs, maybe three, come in if it goes off my glove."

Afterwards, he felt ridiculous for saying that. In the courses he'd taken at North Shore Community College, he'd learned that what you say is sometimes totally different from what you mean. The worst part, in a way, are the little knots of people who actually watch the softball games: not just wives and girlfriends and parents, but teenage girls with cell phones and too much midriff and old men in lawn chairs and the occasional town oddball who has nothing better to do. Everyone, even the girls on their cell phones, understands that Luke is the team's best player, and when he walks toward home plate, bat in hand, he hears people shouting his name. He liked this, at first. But over the years he has often thought of what he'd learned in that psychology class: *sometimes what people say is the opposite of what they mean.* Were they cheers, or jeers? Crushing a softball is so easy for him, like catching trout in an overstocked lake. It's only via the spectacular catch, or inside-the-park home run, that he demonstrates this game can be a challenge for him as well.

And there's some real talent on this team, not just Luke. Just about everyone played high school baseball, and the fielding is crisp, the double plays routine. That's why they were invited to a weekend tournament 300 miles away. And Luke is excited about the trip — perhaps as excited as he's been about anything over the past 10 years. Syracuse is where Luke played the best baseball of his career, where in 1994 the local sportswriters speculated that he would win a spot in the Blue Jays' outfield the following year. It is a city *where people might remember who he is.*

Leslie, who once amazed Luke with her capacity to listen to him, has other things on her mind today, including the mysterious problem with her Toyota: In humid weather, the engine becomes difficult or impossible to re-start, and two days earlier she was stranded with the girls at their day care while Luke was enjoying a beer with one of his softball buddies, his cell phone turned off.

"How about if you take the Toyota today to your game, and leave me the truck?" Leslie says, and Luke, eager to sound conciliatory, offers to catch a ride with one of his teammates.

"That would make things a lot easier for me," Leslie says, and as she carries her empty tea mug into the kitchen, she frowns at the image of Damon in his Yankees cap. "What's he's saying now?" she asks.

"That Red Sox fans are vicious. And that the Sox made him a disgraceful offer."

"I'll say. You'd have to be out of your mind to work for only $8 million a year."

"Oh come on," Luke says with a laugh. "He'll earn every penny of what Steinbrenner is paying him. Just like what's his name...the pitcher who's always on the disabled list."

"Carl Pavano."

"Right. Carl Pavano."

It still amazes Luke that Leslie, the librarian of his dreams who didn't even know there was a professional team in town, now follows baseball more closely than he does. But there's something a little creepy, too, about the way she is in front of the TV night after night, pacing nervously when the Red Sox are threatening to blow a lead. It was Damon who started it all. When he arrived as a free agent in 2002, the team got off to one of its best starts ever. The following year, in the playoffs against Oakland, Leslie was practically chewing on a throw pillow as the A's rallied against Pedro Martinez in the deciding game. Then there was the shallow fly to center field, and Damon racing in, and Damian Jackson, the human cannonball, hustling out, causing what looked like the worst collision in the sport's history. Leslie burst into tears, and Luke himself feared that Damon, motionless on the grass, was dead. But there he was, just five days later, digging in against the Yankees' Roger Clemens. Even Luke had to admit that the guy had balls.

Not that Leslie needed any convincing. By 2004, the year of his Cave Man look, articles about Damon were showing up in the women's magazines that Leslie would bring home from the supermarket. By then, of course, all of New England had lost its mind. It had been difficult for Luke, not having grown up in the area, to understand what all the fuss was about. Of course he knew about the star-crossed history, the sale of Ruth and the home run by Dent, Bob Stanley's wild pitch and Enos Slaughter's scoring from first base on a single — it was in all the books he read. But according to Luke, what people didn't understand was that whether the Red Sox ever won a World Series meant a good deal more to the fans than it did the players. The players, he often reminded Leslie, were just passing through.

But how could anyone not get caught up in what happened in the playoffs that year: the superhuman performance of Ortiz, Schilling's bleeding ankle, Sheffield looking small and helpless as the ball hit by Damon flies high above his head for a grand slam, the Yankees mortally wounded. That night Leslie and Luke achieved a high-flying drunkenness, the box springs in the master bedroom squeaking jauntily, the first time since the All-Star break.

In the sobriety of dawn, however, Luke asked himself why it was that Johnny Damon needed to hit a pennant-winning grand slam before his wife was interested in making love to him.

"Because most of the time you're not here, even when you're here," Leslie had said when he raised the question a few days later. "My God, do you realize how rare it is when we're enjoying something, or even paying attention to something, at the same time?"

"Well," Luke had replied, "what marriage isn't seriously damaged seven years after the wedding day?" It wasn't the answer his wife had wanted.

The urge to depart for Syracuse has become a craving, even though the trip is still a week away. As Leslie turns away from him to intervene in a dispute — Katie is screaming *"It's my horse!"* while Jill tries to wrestle away the plastic animal by its legs — Luke thinks of all those bus rides the year he played for the Sky Chiefs. To Scranton and Rochester and Pawtucket, even all the way to Ohio and Virginia. Guys careful not to get to know each other too well, especially if they played the same position. Hispanics who staked out their corner of the bus, cracking jokes in Spanish until the American players came to suspect that they were the ones being laughed at. A pitcher from Texas reading a pornographic comic book after giving up eight runs in three innings.

Luke knew at the time that this was just a stage to pass through, a moon-bound rocket preparing to drop its booster-engine. When the manager called him into the little office in the visitors' clubhouse in Pawtucket and, grinning crookedly, told him "Don't bother to ride back on the bus with us tomorrow," Luke knew exactly what he meant: The bus that he would be on would travel south through Connecticut, then into Westchester County and on to the Bronx.

It was just another stadium, he had told himself. But then he was in the game, replacing the Blue Jays' Joe Carter, who had a hamstring tighten up on him while hustling out a ground ball in the top of the eighth. And it was not just another stadium. As he jogged toward right field, he gazed at the towering grandstand and wondered just how far up the third of Reggie Jackson's three straight home runs against the Dodgers had landed.

But once the first pitch was thrown, things were no different than in Syracuse or Columbus or any of the half-dozen other stadiums of the International League. Luke rocked on the balls of his feet before each pitch, ready to react. The first batter walked, but the next one lofted a fly ball his way, and Luke trotted in no more than ten yards before the ball sank securely into his glove. It felt good, firing the ball back to the second baseman. He wondered if he'd get a chance to bat in the top of the ninth.

Then Don Mattingly stepped to the plate. The numbers 35, 145, and .324 floated up from a time when Luke was a teenager in Wenatchee, Washington. In 1985, when Luke was in seventh grade, Mattingly was the American League's MVP. He remembered his batting average and his home run and RBI totals for that year because Mattingly was the first player Luke drafted for his Strat-O-Matic team the following June. As he watched Mattingly take the first pitch for ball one, Luke had a remarkably clear image of himself and his friends sitting cross-legged in the grass in front of his parents' house with the Strat-O-Matic cards divvied up by position, Mattingly's card atop the stack of first basemen. As Mattingly fouled off the second pitch, it seemed amazing to Luke that he himself was once a skinny teenager wearing just a pair of jeans and no shoes, gathered with his friends beneath one of those piercingly hot eastern Washington summer days, studying all the SINGLES and DOUBLES, plus a cluster of HOME RUNS, on Mattingly's Strat-O-Matic card. Even if you had no idea who he was, you'd know, just by studying the card, what a good hitter he was.

But why, Luke had asked himself, am I thinking about this right now, right at the moment that Mattingly swings and misses at a breaking pitch? The pitcher had stepped off the mound and Luke stooped over and plucked a few blades of grass and tossed them above him, to better gauge the wind, blowing out gently toward the right field corner. When the pitcher toed the rubber again Luke thought of the defensive coordinator for his high school football team, a former military guy. When someone was trying to explain why he was out of position in the pass coverage, or why he didn't anticipate the pulling guard who cut his legs out from under him, the coach, his face turning red, would shout, "I don't want you to *think!* I want you to *do!*" And wasn't that exactly what an athlete did? You did things so many times that you did them without thinking. Mattingly took ball two, and Luke warned himself to stop having this conversation with himself. After Mattingly fouled back the following pitch, Luke moved a couple steps to his right; with two strikes the hitter was less likely to pull the ball. But the voices from his past kept whispering to him, his father explaining why it would be foolish to turn down the money from the Blue Jays just because he wanted to play both baseball and football at Washington State. Did he understand, his father asked him, what would happen if he injured his knee?

Mattingly fouled off another pitch, and then the count went 3-2. Luke thought: the runner might be running on the pitch, in order to stay out of the double play. If that happens, don't throw all the way to third base; you won't have a play. Be ready, he told himself. Be ready. *And do not think about anything else.* Yet even as he formed this thought Mattingly swung and connected, a hooking line drive headed his way. Luke heard the gasp of the crowd almost as soon as he heard the sound of the bat itself, but as he turned to his right and began to retreat, he knew immediately that he was in trouble. The ball was hooking far more sharply than he had realized. He would have to cross back the other way, accelerate, and hope to stab it before it got over his head. But as he reversed direction he could feel himself losing his balance and then he fell backwards, his cleats in the air and the ball sailing high overhead.

Don't think! Do!

As he got to his feet and chased after the ball, now careening along the wall, he heard a gleefully harsh voice in the stands above him boom out, "Way to fuck things up, rightfielder!" And it made him feel the shame more deeply, that the person who cursed him didn't even know his name.

Leslie's attempt to de-escalate the conflict between Katie and Jill fails, and finally the older girl screams that her mother is always giving Katie what she wants and turns and races past where Luke is sitting, up the stairs and to the bedroom that she and Katie share. Katie is clutching the plastic brown horse so tightly that Luke himself might have trouble prying it from her fingers.

"Well, you were a big help," Leslie tells him once Katie has been mollified.

Luke shrugs. "What can I do when they get like that?"

"You could at least offer me some moral support. Unless, of course, you're already too focused on tomorrow's game."

"Actually, it's the Syracuse trip I've been thinking about."

"For the chance to get away from the rest of us for three days?"

"Yeah, I suppose that's part of it. I promise, once my season's over, that you can go away for a weekend and I'll stay here with the girls. Maybe you and a couple of your friends can go somewhere to watch the Sox on the road."

"That would be nice," Leslie says, and from the look in her eyes Luke can see that there's no sarcasm intended, just the need to get away from the kids for a spell and maybe from him too. He remembers that first night in that scuzzy bar in Lynn, how she listened with rapt attention to his stories of a ballplayer's life on the road. She herself was still living near her dad's place in North Reading at the time and had rarely traveled outside of Massachusetts and New Hampshire. One thing she *had* grasped about professional baseball players was that they had many opportunities to meet young women, and she'd assumed that Luke did this sort of thing all the time, inviting strangers out for drinks after games. It was hard that night to convince her that this was almost as novel an experience for him as it was for her. The girls, the groupies, were around, of course, especially the season he played in Syracuse. They would have their little disposable cameras, taking pictures of certain players and then a few days later asking the player to autograph the print. But Luke told Leslie, without exaggeration, that he had mostly ignored them. "You go out drinking and whatnot, you're out until two or three in the morning, what's that going to do to your concentration at the plate the following evening?" Some of Luke's teammates used to mistake him for a Jesus freak.

"Sure," Luke says now, careful that his own voice sounds sincere, "Go out and enjoy yourself sometime. You deserve it. Just like I do."

He thinks again of the groupies in Syracuse, in particular a dark-haired one that couldn't have been much more than five feet tall. Her name was Lisa Cerone — he remembers this because the Yankees once had a catcher named Cerone, and Luke had asked if they might be related. She had laughed and said that all the men she was related to were Teamsters. Her eyes were large and as dark as her hair, so that the contrast between the whites and the irises was as sharp as a chessboard. Her skin was pale, the eyebrows slender and stark. It was as if Luke was seeing the girl more clearly now than he did then. "How come you don't join us after the games, the way the other guys do?" she had asked, and Luke had smiled somewhat smugly, as if to say, *I have a brighter future than the other guys do.*

He wonders if Lisa Cerone is still living in Syracuse.

"Well," Leslie says breezily, "it seems to me you enjoy yourself quite a lot as it is. I've seen the way those teenagers gaze at you as you strut toward home plate."

"I don't strut. I've never been one to strut. What in hell makes you think I strut?"

"I was only teasing. Don't take yourself so seriously."

This is how it always happens, one of them makes a remark, meant to be in jest, and the other one misunderstands, or willfully misunderstands, and off they go again, in undeclared competition to determine which of them is most deserving of the other's pity.

"And what's it matter if a few teenage girls like to watch me play?" Luke says, his indignation gathering force. "What's it matter if I like that they like to watch me play? How's that any different from you liking to watch Johnny Damon play?"

Leslie sighs, folds her arms. "First of all," she says. "Johnny Damon is on TV. And secondly, he's with the Yankees now."

"As if that makes a difference!" It infuriates Luke that Leslie doesn't pretend to deny that she has had a crush on the man for years.

Katie, still clutching the plastic horse, looks up at her father and her lip starts to quiver. "Christ, Luke," Leslie whispers, "can't we talk about this some other time?"

But Luke wonders if there's even anything to discuss. It was easy enough to see, after all, why his wife would prefer Johnny Boy to him. It wasn't the salary, or the Dunkin' Donuts commercials, or his camera-hogging appearance on *Queer Eye for the Straight Guy*. It wasn't even the flowing hair and the incredible, boyish smile. It was that Johnny Damon didn't sweat the little stuff, or even the big stuff. He didn't worry about the past. He probably didn't even believe in it. How else could he have remained so self-assured, even when things were going badly? In the playoffs against the Yankees he couldn't hit a lick for the first five games. Did it occur to him what would happen if the Red Sox lost again and the people of New England spent the winter assigning blame?

Luke admires Damon, even as he despises him. Glancing at the newspaper article again, he thinks about the reception at Fenway, and wonders if Johnny Boy has started sweating the small stuff now.

The Bet

RACHEL SOLAR

The Red Sox were down three in the series, and technically, I was still married. These are the facts people go crazy about. Oh, and also that he, Freddie, I mean, not Dave, my technical husband, was my best friend. And no, we were not best friends in quotes. We were not the kind of friends who lip kiss after a few too many gin and tonics. We were not "no one is good enough for you — but I am" best friends. We were true, platonic best friends and we had been since B-school. I mean, yes, sure, the first time I laid eyes on Freddie, I did find him attractive. But not "I'm going to do something about it" attractive. More like attractive the way you notice the brownstone in the middle of the block with elegant bones.

There are two kinds of unseasonably warm days in fall. There are the kind that seem out of place and stale, when you want to wear your suede boots for the first time and put the latest Sox season behind you. Banish that awful image of Trot Nixon sitting alone in the dugout surrounded by discarded paper cups, helmet mucked with tar, his head in his hands. And then there are the other kind, the kind where the air has this earthy sweetness and you're not ready to move on yet, and the sun shines on the CITGO sign and the Sox are still in the race — those early dark nights a lifetime away. This was that second kind of Indian Summer day. I was in complete denial about school starting. I was young. I knew in advance that most of my classmates-to-be had already done something with themselves. I didn't know what the hell I was doing, just that my Harvard acceptance letter had bought me some time. Really it was unfathomable — I had the most unworthy 4.0, a bunch of bogus classes cobbled together into a ridiculous Amherst independent study major.

Cringe-worthy now, and I didn't much believe in it at the time, either. (Noah, the latest therapist, would say here that I should be "gentle with myself." He says this often. Another favorite is: "Let go of your expectations." Because if you don't, according to Noah, you'll always be disappointed.)

Anyway, there I was, in the same class as Freddie, the patron saint of hard work. Self-made, aggressive, pursuing a dream, a son of working people, already a businessman who'd sold his first business for a profit, the first to go to college. My first language was therapy; his wasn't even English. Of course I didn't know that, sitting there waiting for my first class to start. All of the seats except one were filled. The professor hadn't arrived yet; there were still a few minutes to go. And except for the odd, hushed small talk, pretty much everyone was silent. Probably thinking about their student loans, and this break in work, and keeping families afloat. I was thinking that for sure I was about to be "found out" — my lack of a scintilla of business school acumen revealed. "You imposter!" my first Harvard professor would say. So we sat there, a bunch of fidgety ticking time bombs in that papery, doom-scented classroom, when, out of the corner of my eye, I saw a blue duffle bag with a Yankees logo on it plop onto the table beside me and a basketball bounce out of it, roll off the table and across the room. Freddie squinted, following the trajectory of the ball, which jostled someone's keyboard (eliciting a death glare) before landing at the feet of a timid looking woman. Freddie glanced at me; we made eye contact for a second, and he cupped a hand to his mouth as if he were about to whisper and then used an unapologetically loud voice instead. "Ten bucks says she throws it back."

I knew good odds when I heard them. I smiled. "Game on."

He stood and lifted his hand in the air, palm up, "Right here, show me what you got." That's when Professor Schoorstein-Brill walked in. The funniest part was, even after the professor stood at the front of the room, for the first few moments, Freddie was still unaware of his presence, trying to get his ball back, holding his hand in the air and pointing to it with the other hand, until Shrill Brill, as he came to be known, said, "Larry Bird, please. This is my classroom. Let us begin, shall we?"

"My apologies, Sir," Freddie said. He did look genuinely sorry.

Class ended, and everyone shuffled off, shell-shocked and stupefied. I pulled out the sports section; we had a ten minute break and there was a story about Nomar's appearance on *Saturday Night Live*. How bogus. What right did he have to be up there, grinning away on TV? He should be catatonic like Trot, not stumbling stiffly through a skit written by a cast member from Lexington, a would-be matinee idol whose glistening, shirtless SI cover had re-cursed us, just when Babe might have stood a chance of fading. Freddie wordlessly slapped a ten on the desk beside me. "I had so much hope for her," he said. "Thought she had a little Swoopes in her. That's my downfall."

"Mistaking meek graduate students for WNBA stars is your downfall?"

"Hope is my downfall. I keep thinking the meek shall inherit the earth."

I laughed. "I'm Leah."

"Freddie," he extended his hand, a decidedly formal gesture compared to everything that had come before. He had a freckle on his palm. It made his hand look friendly, almost mischievous.

"Keep your money, Freddie." I pushed then ten back in his direction. "I have a soft spot for the blindly hopeful. I'm a member of that tribe myself."

"You must be a Sox fan." He smiled but didn't pick up the ten. "Take it. I insist. I'm a man of my word."

It was odd, when I first heard about Karen, I didn't get jealous. I didn't get relieved, either, the way you do when someone you don't find attractive, the kind of person who puts you at risk of an unwanted advance, turns out to be involved with someone. I just felt glad that we could be friends without the burden of this project, something I had to do and worry and wonder about and work on. Usually being friends with someone attractive involved so much activity — wondering if something was going on, wondering if you hoped something was going on, dressing in cute clothes that didn't make you look like you were trying too hard, bantering, dealing with the fact that they then acquire a girlfriend and what that means, etc., but I knew about Karen right off the bat, which I liked. I liked that he didn't pull the girlfriend hiding routine the way some guys do, so suddenly there's this bomb dropping "we."

Karen was a realtor in Manhattan who had an "incredible way with people," which I read to mean that she was not particularly bright — more of a showpiece. I envisioned her selling between stretches in her hot yoga class. And as it turned out she was also — next to the fate part of being assigned the same group — the biggest factor in our friendship developing beyond the average classmate-to-classmate relationship that fades out right after graduation.

On the last day of class before holiday break, Freddie led a rousing game of asshole bingo. We distributed cards marked with the names of all the loudmouth gunners, sabotagers, and sycophants. The code phrase was "a golf course full of elephants." People placed a marker every time one of the gunners ran his mouth. It was a particularly active day, so it was competitive, with lots of almosts. Finally, June Chan won, which presented a challenge, since she was shy, and, in order to demonstrate that she won, rather than BINGO, would have to say the code phrase in front of the class. "Yes, June," Professor Shorstein-Brill looked at a student who had never before volunteered. "Well, Professor," she said, her voice measured (and louder than I would have imagined; clearly she wanted to claim the prize Freddie was offering this week: a complete turkey dinner at Charlie's Kitchen) "this case study presents more problems than a golf course full of elephants."

Freddie and I were still laughing when we left, which I suppose was why I thought he was joking when he said "Kid, come with me to pick out a ring, okay?"

I just laughed more. "You can't marry June just because she won asshole bingo. Although I admit I felt vaguely attracted to her today."

"I'm serious. Help me out, I'm going to propose to Karen over the holiday."

"Wow." I don't think I got a pang in my gut. It was just so unexpected. So maybe I got a small pang. But I recovered quickly and moved right on to the project at hand. We went to EB Horn, and looking back, I'm kind of ashamed to say I picked out a ring I would have wanted, but not necessarily what Karen would have wanted, an estate ring that looked like a flower, with baguettes laid vertically to make the petals and a ruby as the center stone. It wasn't expensive, as far as engagement rings go. But the workmanship was so amazing, I could imagine someone all alone with a pair of tweezers, setting each tiny stone, the vision of the whole brilliant flower always in his mind.

"So what's the plan? How are you going to do it?"

"I was thinking of taking her for a carriage ride in Central Park. Too cheesy?"

"Nah." Personally, I had a vision of a proposal that happened just at one of your regular couple places on a normal night. Like on the couch over Thai food from the neighborhood place. Not at a Sox game with everyone staring, but maybe at Bukowski's after game had ended. After a win, obviously. Still, maybe Karen would appreciate the carriage ride.

"Think she'll say it's too cold for a carriage ride?"

"Of course not."

"You don't know her. She can be kind of high maintenance."

"Ten bucks says she's into it."

"Deal."

As it turned out, I lost ten bucks. Karen said it was cold and a carriage ride was the stupidest idea she ever heard. So Freddie proposed by pushing the ring into her pocket while they were standing there bickering on the sidewalk. When he told me the story, I ran to the bathroom and burst into tears, and I had absolutely no idea why.

I started sleeping with this asshole in our class. Trip Angel was the center square in Bingo, I'm ashamed to say, and had no redeeming virtues except nice delts, a recent negative test for STDs, and an eagerness to please. He wasn't in our section, but I used to see him when I went to games sometimes. Trip played intramural basketball with Freddie. He was the opposite sort of player. Freddie, while not particularly athletic, was quintessentially male out there — dogged, intense, smart with the fakes. Trip, on the other hand, looked all glistening and muscular as he stood around like a deer in headlights. I wondered if his glimmer was the result of actual exertion or some sort of metrosexual body product he bought at Sephora. He was by far the best looking guy in the B-school, a fact that was largely irrelevant as soon as he opened his mouth, but became more so after a few cocktails.

"Seriously, what do you talk about?" asked Freddie, one day in the spring, as we were cutting across the Yard on our way to the T and then to Fenway. The game had already started; once, I'd been able to convince the elder ushers to let us in for free because it was the third inning, so after that we always tried. At the very least the scalpers were more reasonable. Freddie shook his head as a bunch of our classmates made their way to the library, messenger bags slung across their chests. "IT'S FRICKING PASS FAIL," he yelled, at the top of his lungs. I laughed.

"Really — tell me Blum. What the hell are you doing?"

"Entertaining myself."

"You cannot convince me that guy is entertaining."

"Easy for you to say with an import girlfriend. Have you looked at the pickings at this school lately?"

"Have you failed to notice that our boy NEVER passed the ball. And he's a softball idiot too."

"Now that I must take issue with. He's the home run king of intra-league."

"Say it ain't so, Blum."

"What?"

"That is so chick-like of you to be obsessed with the long ball! He's a basepath idiot. Never heard the meaning of the words 'small ball.' He stands there watching his homers like he's fricking Manny Ramirez."

"Hey! Manny only watches dumbfounded for a few minutes. Then he definitely trots."

"I just expected more from you, Kid."

"Maybe there's more to him," I said.

"Yeah. Everyone always thinks a player's going to amount to more than his fair market value. But there's a reason the market values them that way. People have their limitations. Like Byun Hyung Kim is going to get the magic back just because he's with the Sox? How'd that work out for you guys?"

"If he did, though, it would have been the greatest move ever."

"Fricking Sox fans!" I appreciated that Freddie had started to go to non-New York games with me. "We're going to play them in a week," he'd say. "I want to see if this pitcher's stuff is electric." Maybe. But I harbored a little wish that he was starting to fall in love with the Sox just a little, if for nothing more than their unabated hope in the face of so much bad luck and so many near misses. The way they kept believing that it could still happen for them.

We got there for the top of the fourth and I talked a scalper into giving us two nosebleed bleacher seats for ten bucks, which I made back on bets — five because the Sox won and five because Millar wore his socks all the way up. After the game, I walked Freddie home, and then I called Trip and he picked me up on the corner, and I knew as soon as I saw his vapid moon face shining inside the white Beemer that Freddie was right. I didn't know what the hell I was doing.

On the night I met Dave, the Sox were playing their last series against the Yankees. Freddie and I were watching at the Sports Depot in Brighton. I got up to go to the bathroom and I saw blood. My heart started to pound. I had gotten UTIs before, and I thought I might be getting one, but there had never been blood. I associated that with something way more serious. Like cancer.

I called my doctor's after hours service. The nurse called back and told me to go to the emergency room. Freddie took me to the Brigham. It was packed. We watched the rest of the game from there.

Dave was my resident. After a grueling night and a painful Sox loss in extra innings, he said I had a bladder infection. He gave me a prescription and told me to go to the bathroom before and after intercourse. He didn't have a very warm bedside manner; that should have been a warning sign, I guess. But after Trip (I decided that the bladder infection was a sign that I needed to end it with Trip), he seemed pretty appealing. Smart, steady, reliable. A ballast to my craziness.

"So, is someone here to take you home?" Dave asked.

"Yeah. Just a friend from school."

"Which school?"

"Harvard." To this day, I always look down when I say the word.

"Undergrad?"

"Stop, you're making me blush. Business school."

"Ah. Well, I'll let you get back to your boyfriend. He's been here six hours. He's probably exhausted."

"Friend. I don't have a boyfriend."

"Oh. Okay then."

I thought he wanted my number, so I left it with the intake nurse on the way out.

"Smooth move," Freddie said, when he pulled up in front of my place. "Ten bucks said he calls you by tomorrow."

"You're on. And Freddie, thank you."

"Oh, c'mon. Anyone would have done the same."

"No, they wouldn't have. You're my best friend, you know that?" I wanted to tell him a secret, that I had used him as my "in case of emergency," but I was tired and afraid of how he might react. He blushed when I said "best friend," and I hugged him so he didn't have to respond. I could feel his heart beating.

He won the bet. Dave called the next night. He waited until 8:01.

Freddie's dad got pancreatic cancer, and I missed graduation to be with him at the funeral. He told me if he could have me as best man, he would have. But after our weddings, we lost touch for a few years; I don't know why. Maybe it was the distance — he went back to New York and I stayed in Boston. Or maybe it was the excitement around getting started in business, in life, that kept us feeling like we were always running, that our lives were full to the point of brimming over.

Still, we got back in touch around our fifth year reunion (neither of us really wanted to go, and we laughed that we were the only ones we wanted to see). After that, we saw each other a few times a year. Usually he was in recruiting for Wells Fargo or I was meeting with suppliers or going to trade shows for my company — a small business that conceived parties, mostly for children. A few times we watched games from his company seats right behind the third base line. And at one of those games, I was the first person he told that he was getting a divorce. I remember it vividly; it was my first panic attack. He told me, and I ran to the bathroom and couldn't catch my breath. I looked up in the mirror and saw this pale, exposed fear that shocked me. I told myself to breathe, threw water at my face, went back to our seats, and said the kids would be okay when really I didn't know. Later, I met the kids. A girlfriend would never meet the kids — too many issues. But a friend can meet the kids. His kids called me Auntie Leah.

When my own marriage started to fall apart, I borrowed Freddie's litmus test. "I just didn't like coming home anymore," he'd said at that game, his tanned hand wrapped around an cup of beer. With Dave and me, it became a variation of the same, I'd cringe when his key turned in the lock. I just didn't want him coming home. Everything that I loved about him in the first place, his steadiness, his seeming immunity to my charms, the necessary balance I was sure he'd provide, his lack of jealousy — all of it started to wear on me. He had no sense of urgency, which was ironic in an ER doctor, or maybe it was the natural byproduct of being around actual emergencies all day. Even when I told him that if we didn't start making time for each other, paying attention to each other, if we didn't start seeing each other, we'd have to separate, he was still never even mildly stirred up.

Neither Freddie or I had cheated. He proved himself loyal, and not just to the Yankees — an easy thing with dynasty winners; Red Sox loyalty is a far better indicator of a person's ability to be unfailingly loyal — but loyal in the world. And when people ask now — and they often do, believe me — what we have in common, with B-school far behind us now, that's really it. A code of loyalty. A bet's a bet. He was — and is — a man of his word. And I am completely imperfect, but I'm a woman of mine.

When we made The Bet, I'd been separated for a year, and Dave and I had semi-amicably worked out a divorce agreement, which we were waiting for the court to finalize. To any outside observer, I seemed fine. I was running my company and working out and wearing makeup every day and following the Sox. Doing the full spectrum of things you do to show the world you're fine, thinking that, you know, if you do this long enough, eventually it becomes self fulfilling prophecy. So there I was flitting about with my makeup on and my camisole tops, and this party I did all over the papers because it involved a bunch of six-year-olds from Lincoln cleaning up an abandoned playground in Mission Hill and then having an open-to-the public party there with a piñata, and I was going to all these Sox games, justifying the expense because I'd cut marriage counseling short, at a savings of about $200 a week.

And suddenly, there we were down by three, needing to win all four of the next games to make it to the World Series. And in spite of all the flitting around with my $175 jeans and my hands full of martinis that I kept alleging I was ordering for "me and my friends," the truth was I had been crying for a week straight. "I can't believe how easily he's letting me go," I told Noah. "I thought he'd fight for me." Noah shook his head. "Why, because he fought so hard when you were married? Leah, life is not a movie, okay? There are no spotlit epiphany moments, no charging in on horses. There is no soundtrack." At the end of the session, as I stood there wiping my eyes, he said something I'm sure he intended to comfort me. "And I'm sorry about the Red Sox."

"Sorry? Why?" I said. "This is just going to make it that much better when they come back and take the Series." I could tell when I looked at him that I was soundtracking again. But fortunately time was up.

Freddie called when I was driving home. He did that every week, knowing I'd be teary.

"Hi." I didn't have to bite my lip, clear my throat, attempt any of the semi-successful strategies I'd adopted to keep from sounding as if I'd been crying.

"What's up, kid?"

I smiled. The therapist said, actually, that I smiled every time I mentioned Freddie's name. I could tell he was suggesting that I had feelings for him. But I didn't. I smiled when I mentioned his name because he kept promises. He was good to me. Plus he was funny. "Well, apparently, life is not a movie," I said.

"That's what he said tonight?"

"Uh huh," I sniffled.

"I love how you act like life is a movie."

"You do?"

"I do. It's festive."

"That's right. It's festive! What's wrong with festive?"

"Absolutely nothing."

"How was your date?" I remember he took this woman he met at a conference to the last game.

"She's a Mets fan."

"Freddie, you said she was hot! And smart."

He sighed. "There was no spark."

"You can't know that on a first date."

"You can know it in the first five minutes."

I had been on a couple of dates since I was separated, set-ups arranged by friends who thought that all it would take was a little distraction to get this grief period on the fast track. The bond trader who talked about his big boat. The anesthesiologist who had a shirt unbuttoned into his chest hair and got facials at the same place I did. One of them actually stopped watching the Sox midway through the season because they blew their division lead. I'd never date someone so bitter, someone who didn't believe in possibilities, not to mention a fairweather fan. That one became the victim of another of my imaginary migraine headaches. "Well, I liked her," I told Freddie.

"You never met her."

"I liked that she wore a halter top on your first date."

He sighed. "So what are you going to do tonight, kid? You're almost home."

"I don't know. Turn all the lights on. Open a bottle of wine. Eat chocolate for dinner." "And what are you going to do about the Sox?"

"I don't have tickets. I'm going to watch from home."

"No, I mean, have you made a plan for.... I'm worried that...."

"Worried that —" It occurred to me very suddenly what he was worried about. That the Sox would lose and be out of the playoffs and I'd be catatonic. It did make sense. I supposed the therapist was right. I had my hopes up so high. I hadn't allowed myself to really consider that they could be out of it that very night. I just so wanted to keep believing that they'd make it all the way. That everything would be all right.

"I'm worried about you," he said quietly.

"Me too," I said. "Okay, I'm home now. Where are you watching the game tonight?"

"Home."

"Yeah? Is she really plasma screen worthy?"

"Probably not. You inside yet?"

"Yeah. Thanks."

"There's always next year. You know that, right?"

"You just worry about your own team, okay?" I pushed the phone under my chin and opened a bottle of Pinot Grigio.

"They're up by three and about to clinch. So I've got plenty of time to worry about you. I'm worried about our team, kid."

"I thought you were hopeful, like me. What happened, divorce?"

"I'm still hopeful. But I try to be a realist too. I don't expect someone to totally exceed fair market value."

I drained the glass. "Well, I still expect the Sox to win it all."

"I'm sorry, did you say win it all? Kid, you're setting yourself up, okay? Do you understand that statistically speaking. . . ."

"No one has ever done it? Yeah, I understand perfectly. And there's a first time for everything." I took a look around the room, surveying the empty wine glass, the Lindt wrappers, the stacks of celebrity magazines. I felt guilty for loving the Hollywood divorce stories. "I know every statistic, and I still believe."

"And I love your hopefulness, I do, but I'm worried. You're going through a lot right now, and I've been there, and I don't want to see you get hurt."

"Don't worry about me. Worry about yourself. We're going to come back, and win, and then sweep the World Series." I'm finishing another glass, wondering whether I remembered to buy another bottle.

"Sure you will."

"I mean it."

"Look, you're not going to come back, kid. What do I need to do for you to face that? Fine. You come back, sweep the World Series. I'll bet you a thousand bucks. No make it five grand. What the hell, if that happens, I'll quit my job, move to Boston. Hell, we'll get married."

I didn't know if it was the wine, but I thought I could hear my heart thunking against my chest cavity. Really loud. A ball hitting the backstop over and over. I was scared, and it suddenly occurred to me that maybe I wasn't scared to marry Freddie. I wasn't scared because I was divorcing. Maybe I was scared because I didn't want him to say those words as a joke. Maybe I was scared of being a person who wanted to get married again. Maybe I was scared of losing my best friend. Maybe I was scared of his not wanting me. I had an awful feeling in the pit of my stomach. Maybe Freddie was right about being too hopeful, about leaving yourself vulnerable. Suddenly I started to think seriously about the outcome of the game.

Too much time had passed (I hoped it seemed like more in my head than it actually was in real time) and I still hadn't mustered anything to say. "You have to wait for me to get a divorce," I finally said, quietly.

One thing about Freddie: he always hears me, even with a bad connection, even if I can only muster a whisper. "You've got a deal." He let this laugh of his go. And I was remembering some time in B-school when we were laughing — it was a vague memory, maybe it was after exams — and how his whole face would engage, and how for a moment I had this feeling, you know those once in a while feelings, where you forget where you are and just feel, I don't know, calm. Like you could conceivably let go, let the chips fall where they may. Like you could conceivably just be happy.

"Okay then. It's a bet."

"Oh my god. Listen to me, kid. Okay? I am just trying to show you how unrealistic this is," he said. His voice had popped back into place, and he sounded as serious as I'd ever heard him. "I love that hopeful spirit about you, I do. I don't want you to lose all the movie you. But it just...."

"Just what?"

"It just rips me up to see you get let down."

"Well, don't you worry about me. Why don't you go back to whatshername? They're announcing the lineup."

When Freddie and I met for a drink at Bukowski's the night after Game Four of the Series, he put the ring on the table in front of me without a word. "Freddie..." I said. But he cut me off.

"Look, I was wrong," he said. "About a lot of things. Sometimes people do surprise you in a good way. Sometimes people are more than their fair market value. Look at David fricking Ortiz."

I smiled. I had tears in my eyes.

"And I cannot believe what I am about to say." He put his hand over mine, and I felt a shiver. I could hardly breathe. "I'm a man of my word. And a bet's a bet."

I nodded my head. "Freddie, it's okay...." I pushed the ring toward him just a little and tried to smile.

"No, wait. Kid — Leah. I'm trying to tell you that I realized in the fifth ALCS game that I was rooting for the Sox."

I knew right then and there that he'd make an excellent husband.

Kicking In

BILL NOWLIN

"What would it be like if the Sox ever won it all?"

"It might take away our soul. Boston would never be the same."

"I know what you mean, but I guess I'd like to find out. Put it to the test. The scientific approach — let's see them win the World Series, and then see what happens to our soul."

"Yeah, right. Like it's ever going to happen."

"I'd give my left arm for it . . . just once in my life . . . I dunno. . . ."

"I can't take it any more. Two years in a row now. Aaron Boone last year and now Schilling's gone and. . . .19 to 8? It's humiliating. The worst of it is, it's gonna be another year of that sick Yankees singsong '19 . . . 18.' I don't know if this one will ever heal. There's nothing more to be done. I've tried everything, pulled out all the stops. . . ."

Richie left a bit of his sub behind him and walked out of the shop, mumbling his goodbyes. He kicked an empty paper cup and crossed the street, walking home. What would it take? He'd been a fan since grade school, watched every game he could on TV, got to the park a couple of times a year. Richie had even worked as an extra in *Fever Pitch* just to get into Fenway. They let me down again, he thought, suddenly enraged. Dragging up on the curb, he saw the newspaper headline in the vending box next to the mailbox: SOX SLAUGHTERED.

Man!! Fury redoubled, he lashed out with a mindless kick at the *Herald* box, but missed, tumbled forward, and stumbled awkwardly, the side of his head slamming into the sharp corner of the hard metal box.

A flash of heat, then a flash of cold, and he knew . . . just knew . . . he was dying. "Could a death be any cornier?" — the flickering thought flitted across his mind. "And now I'll never know the feeling. They never won it in my lifetime."

The morgue worker settled the body onto the gurney, Richie's Sox cap bloodied and askew. "Jeez, poor guy. What a way to go."

"Yeah, well at least he won't have to see tonight's game," the cop said in his usual sardonic manner.

While Roberts scored the tying run in the background, a voice over the phone to surgery said, "Yeah, universal donor. Little red heart on the license. We confirmed with next of kin. I can have it ready in the morning."

Dr. Morgan told Schilling, "I think it looks good. The tendon's a little inflamed now, of course, but it should settle down in a couple of days. I'll tell Wallace you might be able to do some mound work on Friday."

"A cadaver, though? I still can't get my mind around that," Schilling said, shaking his head. "Poor bugger."

"Richie woulda loved it. Man, could anything be worse? I mean, he's dead, yeah, it sounds stupid but for him to go the way he did and just a week before...."

"The guy lived and breathed the Sox. He bled Red Sox blood. He was always saying he woulda liked to see what it was like, what they city would be like if they won it all. I hear there's three million people at the parade."

"Julia, this is so terrific. I never thought I'd see the day. In fact, I never thought I'd see again. I don't know who it was — they don't give you all the details, but I know it was a young man. To think that I came out of the cornea transplant two days ago, just in time to see Foulke flip the ball to Mientkiewicz. And now this wonderful parade."

"The rain's mixing with your tears, Steph; I'm so happy for you. Whoever that guy was, he sure kicked in big time."

The Ten Fenway Commandments

SARAH GREEN

Hear, O Fenway Faithful, the statutes and judgments which I speak in your ears this day, that ye may learn them, and keep, and do them.

I am the Team thy Red Sox, which have brought thee out of the Curse of the Bambino, out of the house of bondage.

1. Thou shalt have no other Teams before me.

2. Thou shalt not buy unto thee any other team's graven merchandise, or any bobblehead of any player that is in Canada above, or that is in the States below, or that is in the States to the West: Thou shalt not bow down thyself to them, nor root for them: for I the Team thy Red Sox am a jealous Team, visiting the iniquity of the fathers upon the children unto the third and fourth generation of them that hate me (or them that selleth players to finance Broadway musicals); And showing mercy unto thousands of them that root for me, and keep my commandments.

3. Thou shalt not jeer the name of the Team thy Red Sox in vain; but the Team shall hold him guiltless that cheereth and maketh a joyful noise unto the Team.

4. Remember the season, to keep it holy. Two-hundred and three days shalt thou labor, and do all thy work: But one-hundred and sixty-two days are the game days of the Team thy Red Sox: in them thou shalt not do any work, thou, nor thy son, nor thy daughter, thy assistant, nor thy cleaning lady, nor thy dog, nor thy cat, nor any of thy goldfish, nor thy stranger that is within thy cul-de-sac: For

in the offseason, the Team made offense and defense, the pitching rotation, and all that in them is, and played the season: wherefore the Team blessed the season, and hallowed it.

5. Honor thy hot dog vendor and thy beer man, as the Team thy Red Sox hath commanded thee; that thy season may be prolonged, and that it may go well in October, in the Fenway which the Team thy Red Sox giveth thee.

6. Thou shalt not kill for season tickets.

7. Thou shalt not have pennant fever for two teams at once.

8. Thou shalt not steal away from thy seat until the final out hath been recorded. It is easier for a camel to pass through the eye of a needle than for a businessman to stay nine innings on Opening Day.

9. Thou shalt not bear false witness against thy umpire. Let them alone: they be blind leaders of the blind. And if the blind lead the blind, both shall fall into the dugout.

10. Thou shalt not covet the Yankees' stadium, thou shalt not covet the Yankees' payroll, nor their farm system, nor their manager, nor their free agents, nor their Championship rings, nor anything that is the Yankees.

These words the Team spake unto all Red Sox Nation, with a great voice over the loudspeaker: and they trembled, and said unto the Team, "So good! So good! So good!" And the Team wrote the commandments into two scoreboards and delivered them unto yet.

Contributors

STEVE ALMOND is the author of two story collections, *My Life in Heavy Metal* and *The Evil B.B. Chow*, the non-fiction book *Candyfreak*, and the novel (with Julianna Baggott) *Which Brings Me to You*. His next book is a collection of essays, to be published in 2007 by Random House.

AL BASILE grew up in a park in Haverhill, Mass. He is a singer-songwriter who began his musical career as a cornet player with Roomful of Blues in 1973, and has worked with the Duke Robillard Band since 1990. He has five solo CDs out under his own name.

DAVID DESJARDINS is a copy editor at the *Boston Globe*. He lives in Arlington, Mass., with his wife, Cathie, and his son, Dylan. David's Red Sox mania dates back to the days of Monbouquette, Radatz, and Dr. Strangeglove himself, Dick Stuart.

MITCH EVICH is the author of *The Clandestine Novelist*, a semi-autobiographical novel. He is working on a collection of short stories, several of which have sports-related themes.

BOB FRANCIS is a May 2006 Graduate of Gordon Conwell Theological Seminary "Center For Urban Ministries Education," with a Master of Arts in Urban Ministries. With God's help he hopes to pastor a church. Bob considers the Sox to be the heartbeat of New England, and loves to experience the highs and lows of being a fan.

TIMOTHY GAGER is the author of two books of short fiction and two of poetry. He has a daughter "Sweet Caroline" and a son Gabe.

HENRY GARFIELD is the author of five published novels, including *Tartabull's Throw*, from which the selection herein is excerpted. His work has appeared in numerous magazines and newspapers on both coasts. He lives and writes in Maine, and dabbles in songwriting under the name Hank Williams Garfield. Visit his website at hwgarfield.com.

TRACY MILLER GEARY's stories have appeared in numerous literary magazines, as well as the previous edition of *Fenway Fiction*. She is still trying to come to terms with the idea of Johnny Damon in a Yankees uniform.

SARAH GREEN is a freelance writer and sports columnist for the *Boston Metro*. Sarah is a lifelong resident of New England and a devout congregant of the Fenway Faithful.

Providing the first inkling of evidence that Red Sox Nation were the cause behind the Big Bang, expanding and contracting geographically, MATT HANLON's wife allowed them to spring back to Massachusetts, where he secretly has their one-year-old son scheduled for Tommy John surgery in '08 so he can help the Sox rotation out sooner rather than later. His frequent walks by Fenway Park with the child are not, he swears, intended to get him "noticed" by the lazier Sox scouts.

MARY KOCOL is an art photographer and filmmaker in Somerville, Mass. You can see more of her work on her website: http://www.KocoMotion .com. Gallery NAGA, run by "wicked huge" Sox fans, represents her photography in Boston. Mary is still partying after the 2004 Red Sox World Series victory.

DAVID KRUH's most recent book, *Scollay Square*, is his second effort on Boston's bygone entertainment district (the first was *Always Something Doing: Boston's Infamous Scollay Square*). He also co-authored *Presidential Landmarks* with his father Louis and *Building Route 128* with Yanni Tsipis. David's columns have appeared in a number of publications including the *Boston Globe, Boston Herald, Boston Magazine*, and *Yankee Magazine*. In 2001 *The Curse of the Bambino Musical* premiered at the Lyric Stage Company of Boston, and eventually broke all the box office and attendance records for the theatre during its extended run.

STEVEN BERGMAN is an award-winning, published playwright, who has also composed the scores for a number of other musicals and motion pictures.

LENORE MYKA has been a recipient of a City of Somerville Arts Council grant and was the Corrine Steele Fellow at the Millay Colony of the Arts. She lives and writes in Somerville, Mass..

BILL NOWLIN is author of more than a dozen books on the Red Sox and Sox-related matters. Bill is a co-founder of Rounder Records of Burlington, Mass., and current vice president of the Society for American Baseball Research.

ELIZABETH PARISEAU has worked as a reporter for several Massachusetts newspapers and publishes a blog, Cursed and First, devoted to the Red Sox and Patriots.

JENNIFER RAPAPORT's short fiction has appeared in *Quarterly West* and *Paragraph*. Jen is happy to report that for her there was no negative fall-out from the '04 Championship.

RON SKRABACZ grew up in East St. Louis, Illinois. He became a lifelong Red Sox fan in 1967 because of Carl Yastrzemski and his Polish heritage. To emulate Yaz he created the nickname "Skraz" and began wearing No. 8 on all his baseball and softball jerseys. His greatest satisfaction as a Red Sox fan is that his father and fellow Red Sox fan, Ed Skrabacz, got to see them win a championship before he died in November 2005. Ron is a budget manager for AT&T and writes a weekly sports column for the *Daily Herald*, a suburban Chicago newspaper. He and his wife of 27 years, Becky, have three children, Nicole, Sarah, and Jake (a White Sox fan). You can spot Ron by his SKRAZ 8 license plate.

RACHEL SOLAR is the author of *Number Six Fumbles* and co-author of *Table Talk: A Savvy Girl's Guide to Networking*. According to her son, Jack, who is adopted from Korea, there are three teams in baseball: the Yankees "from out of town," the "White Red Sox" from Chicago, and the Red Sox "from Korea."

CECILIA TAN lives in Cambridge, Mass., and for five years lived two blocks from Fenway Park. A writer and editor by trade, she writes fiction of many kinds (erotica, science fiction, etc.) and nonfiction about her many passions, of which baseball is the chief one. She is the author of *Fifty Greatest Yankee Games* and co-author with Bill Nowlin of *Fifty Greatest Red Sox Games*, and she edited *The Fenway Project* and *'75: The Red Sox Team That Saved Baseball* with Bill. She considers the Yankees her childhood sweetheart and the Red Sox her troubled roommate. Find out more at http://www.ceciliatan.com

MICHELLE VON EUW's stories have appeared in *Elysian Fields Quarterly, Aethlon: The Journal of Sports Literature,* and the *Charles River Review*. She teaches writing at her undergraduate alma mater, George Washington, and the University of Maryland, where she earned her MFA. She's been a Red Sox fan since before she can remember, and, like Caroline, considers Fenway Park her favorite place on earth. A sports editor for Intrepid Media, Michelle currently resides with her husband just outside Washington, where she is currently at work on a collection of stories about women and baseball.

JONATHAN WINICKOFF is a Pediatrician at Massachusetts General Hospital and a lifelong Red Sox fan. He would like to thank his son Sam for listening to various iterations of the Haiku while riding on the C line together.

Call for Submissions

Have you written a piece of fiction inspired by the Boston Red Sox? If so, you are invited to submit it for possible inclusion in a future anthology. Short stories in any genre, play and novel excerpts, poems, and the like are all welcome. If you'd like more information, please contact the editor at adampachter@yahoo.com or send your completed story to:

Rounder Books
Attn: *Fenway Fiction* Series
One Rounder Way
Burlington, MA 01803

We look forward to hearing from you!

About the Editor

ADAM EMERSON PACHTER is the author of the novel *Ash* (ISBN 0-89754-192-8) and numerous short stories, as well as the editor of the first *Fenway Fiction* (Rounder, ISBN 1-57940-119-8). He lives with his wife and daughter in Arlington, Mass., and vows to continue compiling future *Fenway Fiction*s as long as the good stories keep coming in.

Short Stories from Red Sox Nation

Edited by Adam Emerson Pachter

FENWAY FICTION

The Boston Red Sox have inspired generations of writers, and not just those newspaper scribes whom Ted Williams called the "knights of the keyboard." The Sox have been integral players in fiction as well. They provided atmosphere and context in films such as *Field of Dreams* and *Good Will Hunting* and contributed key characters to the novels of Robert Parker and Stephen King.

Although the actual history of the Red Sox has often been stranger than fiction, until *Fenway Fiction* was published there had never been an all-fiction anthology devoted to stories about the Sox. Penned by novelists, playwrights and ardent fans, these 17 tales take the reader on an imaginative journey around the basics of humor, history, and heartache. Within these pages you'll discover how one fan's marriage is impacted when Manny Ramirez accepts an invitation to dinner, learn the story behind Johnny Damon's beard, take a musical tour through the Curse of the Bambino, and try to solve a murder mystery set during the strike-shortened 1981 season. After reading *Fenway Fiction*, you'll never look at Boston's beloved baseball team quite the same way again.

CONTRIBUTORS:

Skye Alexander	Jeff Parenti
Steven Bergman	Sam and Christina Polyak
Mitch Evich	Jennifer Rapaport
Tracy Miller Geary	Andy Saks
Matthew Hanlon	Tom Snee
David Kruh	Rachel Solar
Bill Nowlin	Cecilia Tan
Adam Emerson Pachter	Robert Weintraub
Elizabeth Pariseau	Jonathan P. Winickoff